Troy and Aaron Mayer, identical twins separated at the age of two, lived wildly different lives. Aaron struggled to take care of their alcoholic, gambling-addicted mother, while Troy, raised by their father, experienced a life of luxury.

After years of silence, Troy asks to see Aaron. When Aaron arrives at his brother's boat, he finds a note instead and suspects suicide. In his farewell note, Troy offers Aaron his car, his money, and his life of riches.

On the run from loan sharks, Aaron slips easily into this mirrored life. But everywhere he turns he discovers somebody Troy devastated, including his handsome husband, Dave Alvarez. Pulled into his brother's life of crime, Aaron is set up for a fall, but he's too strong to shatter.

This book was previously published as Mirrors.

Mirror Image
Copyright © 2020 A.J. Llewellyn and D.J. Manly
ISBN: 978-1-4874-2911-9
Cover art by Martine Jardin

Published by eXtasy Books Inc or
Devine Destinies, an imprint of eXtasy Books Inc

Look for us online at:
www.eXtasybooks.com or www.devinedestinies.com

Mirror Image
Mirror Image Book 1

By

A.J. Llewellyn and D.J. Manly

DEDICATION

Dedicated to all our faithful readers.

CHAPTER ONE

The boat rocked on the water as if it were made of paper. The wind swirled around him in a haze and whipped his fair hair around his face. Desperately, he tried to see through waves rising and falling around him. *Troy? Troy?* A mix of anxious anticipation and dread filled his rapidly beating heart as he scanned the water. The boat took on a life of its own and attempted to wrestle him over the side, propelling him into the unknown depths. *Come. Come with me, Aaron.* A face looked up at him in the swirling water. It was *his*.

Fourteen months earlier

The voice on the other end of the phone couldn't have sounded more estranged from him if it had been a person doing a marketing survey. It took him a few minutes to recognize who it was. And it shouldn't have. It was light with an underlying lyrical baritone, so like his own voice.

"Aaron? Don't you know who this is?"

Yes, I know.

"How are you?" He paused. "I was sorry to hear about Mom."

Aaron perched on the side of the sofa. *Make words, fool.* "Yeah, well, you know."

"So I'm thinking, maybe we should get together? When was the last time?"

Was there a last time?

He didn't wait for an answer. "I really did want to make it to the funeral. Dad and I were both in Europe on a buyer's trip at that time. Wow, the summer of two-thousand-ten was

1

really a busy one."

Mother died in the summer of two-thousand-nine. "How is Dad?"

"Good. He's in Spain with his newest wife, number four. A fashion model, legs up to there. You know Dad."

No, I don't know Dad.

"So, we have a birthday coming up in a week, twenty-seven, can you believe it? How about you come down here to Bel Air and we go out for the day on Dad's yacht? I mean, I don't know if you're working or what. We can do it when you're off work. I pretty much make my own hours. It would good to see each other, right? Aaron?"

"Yeah, I . . . I guess."

"Okay, so how about Saturday?"

"Ah, Saturday . . . I'd have to check and . . ."

"Aaron, you act like you don't want to see me."

"I just wonder why now?" There, it was out. All this time, Troy had never even bothered to pick up the phone, ask how he was doing, how Mother was doing. Troy was sitting pretty down there in Bel Air, living the good life, and he had been up here in the shit, struggling to survive. All the lost years trying to scrounge up enough cash to get Mom into yet another rehab clinic.

"Why *not* now?" Troy came back with.

They were twins, identical. They'd been separated since the age of two. Their parents were ill-suited from the onset. Aaron would never understand what attracted Darren Mayer, who'd come from generations of wealth, to the shy, little working-class girl from the Bronx. Sarah Stein was like a fish out of water in high society and her Jewish heritage didn't sit well with Darren's protestant family.

Talk about a parent trap.

After the twins were born, Sarah fell into a deep depression. Her young husband was given the import business to run. She was displaced from her beloved New York City and her family.

Sarah couldn't seem to fit in with high society. Darren began to go out a lot, leaving her alone. She started drinking. Darren hired a nanny to look after the boys and disconnected from her. The long business trips and numerous affairs didn't help and finally Sarah tried to take her own life. Darren waited until she got out of the hospital, then he left her.

Darren's father insisted he take one of the boys when he filed for divorce. Darren was an only child, and his father was concerned about the family line. In exchange for taking one of the boys, Sarah accepted the big house in Beverly Hills, and one lump sum of money. Within five years, she had squandered the money and was forced to sell the house. Eventually they were destitute, relying on food stamps and the kindness of strangers. Sarah's family begged her to come back home to New York, but she was too proud, and Aaron believed she couldn't bear to let her family see what she'd become.

An assembly line of strangers went in and out of their three-room apartment in the mostly Hispanic neighborhood of Mar Vista. The strangers would bring booze, in exchange for sex. Sometimes they'd give her money, and Aaron would sit out on the fire escape until they left. Then, if he was lucky, he could grab the money before she came to, and he'd buy groceries before she could get to the liquor store.

He eventually grew up and left her. He moved as far away as his work as a landscaper would let him. His life in Los Osos, the 'valley of the bears,' on California's central coast hadn't been bad until Sarah started fleecing him. She'd forged his signature on loans, secured credit cards she'd diverted to her flop house down in East LA. It was still a nightmare untangling himself from the mess.

It didn't help when he learned that many parents wrecked their kids' credit through identity theft.

When her liver failed, and she was dying, it was almost a

relief. Aaron left a message with the secretary of his father's company, but he never came to visit. Not even Troy showed up for their mother's funeral.

It still hurt remembering how she'd vanished from yet another expensive, futile trip to a lockdown facility called Promises.

Yeah. Lots of those. Piecrust promises. Easy to make; so easily broken.

She'd somehow managed to escape over the wall with the help of a ridiculous, drug-hungry celebrity. The actor had gone on a cocaine-fueled binge chronicled by the media whilst Sarah had quietly checked herself into a cheap motel on Sunset Boulevard, drinking herself to death.

Aaron had found her with the aid of his debit card, which she had stolen. Not her finest moment, to be sure. She lay in the small bed of her hotel room, her legs ballooned to three times their usual size, her skin a frightening color. Aaron had paid a doctor who didn't know her to come to the hotel. He'd hoped the handsome stranger could convince Sarah to allow herself to be hospitalized.

"Her vital organs are shutting down fast," the doctor had said. "Her own body is turning against her. It's filling with toxins, hence the swelling in her legs."

It took another twenty-four hours to convince Sarah to get medical help. The handsome doctor came back to help facilitate her journey via an ambulance. Aaron couldn't fail to notice the relief on the hotel staff's faces. The maid told him half their clients checked in and never checked out again. They'd recently had a former pop star die after a drunken binge. He'd checked in with a friend's help and according to the staff was quiet and respectful.

He drank until his heart stopped. There was no ID on him except for a piece of paper in his pocket with the shaky words, *I am Johnny Lee.*

To Aaron's dismay, his mother was headed to a hospice,

not a hospital. She'd lit up at the prospect and happily signed the Do Not Resuscitate form required to admit her to the facility that spelled the end of her road.

Welcome to the Hotel California.

Promises.

"They'll keep me sedated and I will pass from this life," she'd told Aaron. "I can't wait."

She was dead in two days, Aaron her only visitor. The hospice staff called to tell him she'd passed at four o'clock in the morning.

"She didn't suffer," they said.

Yeah, but I did.

He'd made all the arrangements for her funeral. She'd looked grotesque at the end and it still wounded him that he'd had to handle it all without any help.

"Are you miffed at me for not coming to the funeral, Aaron?"

Aaron was hardly aware that he was still holding the phone. "What did you say? Sorry."

"Did you drop the phone?"

"No. I'm here."

"I asked if you were miffed at me for not coming to the funeral. You know, I never felt very close to her."

"How could you? You didn't even know her."

"Dad told me some stuff about her though."

"I'm sure he did." Aaron closed his eyes.

"So, how are things with you?"

Should I tell him? Should I really tell him about the trouble I'm in? The loan sharks? How this time they'd hurt me good? Maybe he can help me. Troy has money. He could lend me some. Should I ask?

"I . . . Do you want the truth, or do you want bullshit?"

"The truth."

"Well, ah . . . I'm in a little bit of trouble."

"What kind of trouble? Trouble with the police?"

"Loan sharks. I need money."

"How much money?"

"More than I got, a few grand."

"Okay. I can help you with that."

Aaron was skeptical. "Why are you being so nice to me?"

"You're my brother. So, you'll come for sure on Saturday?"

He was stunned. Troy was going to help him. "Okay. You know I really appreciate you helping me out. I'll pay you back, every cent."

"You don't have to. I know where you live. There's a marina in Morro Bay. I'll have our boat pick you up."

"Just tell me what pier. I'll be there."

"Pier number ten, and ah . . . let's say nine in the morning?"

"I'll be there." He hung up and realized that he hadn't even said goodbye.

Troy has a boat and I'm on my last packet of Twinkies . . .

He walked to the window and pushed aside the moth-eaten curtain. He scanned the street. It was early yet. They'd be coming. He just had to lay low until he could get the cash. The last time he'd asked for more time, they'd broken two of his fingers. He'd been unable to work, and the bills kept coming, not to mention the compound interest on the loans he stupidly took to try and handle his outrageous debt . . . He dreaded to think what they'd break this time.

Aaron was nervous about seeing his twin Saturday morning. He'd spent a scary couple of days avoiding the loan sharks. He'd actually slept in Elfin Forest in his sleeping bag. All the time he'd been in Los Osos and he'd never visited the forest. He would have been charmed by the air parade of monarch butterflies had he not been petrified of homicide.

It had been too dangerous to drive his car to the forest and he'd told nobody of his plans. Better to leave his car at home. The goon squad would know it if they saw it out and about.

He took the tourist van that cost a quarter, then hiked a mile into the woods. For two nights he'd listened for marauding bears . . . the humankind and the animalkind. He'd spent the days wandering deeper into the forest, thrilled when he'd found a crumpled five-dollar note in the campground showers.

Early Saturday, he took the bus down to the main road and passed his street.

His car sat in his driveway, torched.

Holy crap . . .

He had persuaded Jake, one of his last friends left in the sleepy beach town, to drive him to Morro Bay. His stomach was in such knots he wondered if he'd swallowed some of those forest butterflies.

"Thanks," he told Jake, who'd lent him a clean shirt and slipped him a few bucks. He tried to decline, but Jake insisted.

"Here, I think you'll need it."

Aaron climbed onto the boat that was docked in the pier as his buddy took off.

The boat was called *The Promise.*

How apt.

There was no one on deck. "Troy?"

He ducked his head in the door and climbed down the steps to the cabin below. The floor was covered in royal blue carpeting. There was a large screen television on one wall, a small galley kitchen to the side. He walked to the stainless-steel counter where an ice bucket sat cradling a bottle of expensive champagne. The ice had melted. There was an envelope propped up against the champagne bucket. On the front was written: *To Aaron. Welcome to your new life.*

Aaron narrowed his eyes and looked around. He walked toward the door which stood open on the other side of the room and peeked in. There was a double bed with a white duvet and a small oak bureau. The bed showed no sign of having been slept in.

Maybe Troy hadn't arrived yet. Maybe he should just wait but he was still holding the envelope. Perplexed, he opened it and took out the note.

Hello brother,

By the time you read this, I'll be gone. It's not important where. In fact, if I knew that, I'd have to answer an age-old question. Everything you need to start your new life is in the top drawer of the bureau in the bedroom. Don't feel guilty. I inherited this life by chance. It was the flip of the coin. It might have been yours. Now it is. I know it will be strange at first, but it will solve all your problems, and it's your turn. Good luck, brother.
Love, Troy

How long does it take to step into the life of someone else? When you look identical to the other, it's instantaneous, but not as simple as one might imagine.

Aaron didn't know anything specific about Troy's life except that he worked with their father in the import business and was filthy rich. How in the hell was he supposed to be him, not to mention . . . where *was* Troy? Had he committed suicide? It certainly sounded that way in his letter.

When Aaron opened the top drawer of Troy's bureau, he found a driver's license, credit cards, bank books, keys, and a recent photo. Aaron stared at it. Yes, they were identical, same sandy blond hair, same blue eyes, both five eleven, about one seventy. Aaron wore his hair longer though he didn't have the fancy haircut. If this was going to work, he'd have to remedy that.

He also found an agenda which listed what Troy had to do each day. Meetings, medical appointments, picking up laundry, paying the staff, meeting someone called 'Matt' for lunch the next day. It seemed that Troy was a very organized man; something that Aaron wasn't.

Aaron reread the note. *By the time you read this, I'll be gone.* Why would he kill himself? He had it all. Should he call the police?

A sudden realization fell over him. Aaron raced up the steps onto the dock and frantically searched the calm blue waters. He half-feared finding his brother floating, then hoped he would . . . and do what? *Closure. I would have closure. I would know he's dead. But do I want him to be dead or alive?*

I . . . don't know.

He roamed the boat, checking the water as far as he could see. He had no idea how to operate a boat. What was he supposed to do now? Troy wouldn't have thrown himself into the water here while the boat was docked, would he? Was his brother *really* dead? Why would he choose this time to kill himself?

It was all so . . . strange. His whole life he'd veered between hating his twin and hoping for a reconciliation that involved the two of them being rich and happy. Instead, Aaron had struggled regardless of his efforts to get himself above water.

Don't feel guilty. I inherited this life by chance. It was the flip of the coin. It might have been mine. Now it is.

It was true. He wasn't stealing a life. He was stepping into a life that he had just as much of a right to have. Perhaps it was this fact alone that allowed him to go ahead with it, that and the loan sharks who waited for him back home.

Aaron returned to Troy's bedroom. He sat there on the bed most of the day and contemplated what he was about to do. If he did this, Aaron Mayer would just disappear, and along with him his troubles, his mistakes, and his past. It was his chance to start over. Troy had handed him a new life for whatever reason. He had to take it.

Aaron grabbed all the papers he would need. He picked up Troy's car keys with the car starter attached and left the boat. The sun had gone down, and it was cooler than normal. He headed for the parking lot and pointed the car starter in the direction of the parked vehicles. A sparkling blue Corvette roared to life while its headlights slowly unveiled. "Nice."

Aaron inhaled the smell of new leather when he slipped behind the wheel as if it were a drug. He adjusted the rear-view mirror and rolled forward, slowly.

He drove down the coast, his hands shaking. He had never driven anything so lovely. Was it a dream? It all felt so . . . illicit. He was almost in a trance all the way to Santa Barbara. Maybe it was real, that luck could change, and good things could sometimes happen after a lifetime of living under a dark cloud.

It was a shock to see the old-fashioned freeway signs announcing that he'd reached Santa Barbara. He glanced at the dashboard clock. He'd made the eighty-nine-mile drive in a little over an hour. The cops hadn't busted him. Maybe his luck was already changing. He shoved the picture of his twin into his pocket and stopped at the first hair salon he could find on State Street.

Standing at the reception desk, he waited only a moment for a hip-looking stylist to come forward to ask if he had an appointment, Aaron said, "No. I just need a cut." He took out the picture. "It's a cut I had before. Can you do that?"

"Of course," the young man smiled. "Very becoming. Unfortunately, I have no place for you now. We are just about to close. If you come back . . ."

"No," Aaron said. "I can't. I have to get it cut now. Ah . . ." he added when the stylist gave him a curious look, "it's driving me nuts and . . . I have a meeting tonight. Please, look." He took out his brother's credit card. "Whatever you charge here for a haircut, I'll pay double."

"Seventy is the usual price. So let's say one-forty, plus the tip of course."

Aaron was aware of the man staring at his bandaged fingers that for some reason had started to throb. He kept them on his lap and drew a deep breath. Let the fun begin.

"Of course," Aaron replied. "How about an even two hundred?"

"Let's get started."

CHAPTER TWO

It wasn't difficult to find the location of the seven-bedroom house his brother lived in. The onboard navigation had been pre-programmed with the Bel Air address. It was eerie to get back into the vehicle with his new haircut and the mechanical navigation voice telling him how to get back on the freeway to Bel Air.

Aaron drove, unable to stop thinking about the fact that his now-destroyed Ford Taurus had forever been on its last legs. The windows and the driver side door didn't open, and the transmission slipped constantly. What a dream to be cruising along the ritzy part of Sunset to his brother's estate, through the gated Bel Air community.

He experienced a small moment of panic at the guard gate. Leaning on the window button, he marveled at how smoothly it operated. The Taurus's window had been stuck since the day he bought it at auction. Aaron recognized the ornate wrought-iron gates from television. His brother had been interviewed in his house last year for a show about luxury homes, because it was filled with fancy antiques. Troy had told the interviewer that the house had originally been built for his father's second wife, but that Troy decided to keep it when they divorced.

"Good evening, Mr. Mayer," the guard said, opening the gate. "The meeting has already started, I'll let Mr. Watanabe know you're home."

Who in the hell is Mr. Watanabe and what meeting is he talking about?

Aaron smiled and nodded as he angled the car inside the gates. From the rearview mirror, he could see the guard picking up a phone inside his little cubicle. The gate swung sedately closed behind him. Aaron moved forward, aware of his fingers sweating against the steering wheel leather.

Where in hell was the house? Panic prickled at him. He'd look like an idiot if he began circling the giant, curving road. He blinked for a moment, staring ahead. It looked like something out of *Desperate Housewives* . . . what was it called? Wisteria Lane. He'd expected mansions and yes, they were there . . . but what the fuck? Which way did he go? Left or right?

He glanced back in the rearview mirror and saw that the gate guard was staring at him. *Oh, spiffing.*

Just as he'd decided to turn right, the onboard navigation system startled him.

"Turn right then one hundred yards ahead, turn right on St. Cloud Road."

"Thank you," he said, then rolled his eyes at himself . . . *thanking a damned computer now!*

The house stood on a plateau above a steep incline, surrounded by trees. It was a sprawling Spanish style, with black grated windows and doors. Rose bushes lined the path leading to the front door and there was a small fountain with a pond. A Greek-like statue of an angel peed water into the reservoir.

Did Troy park in his garage? He noticed an old truck parked in the driveway and turned the car around in front of the house. When Aaron got out, a middle-aged Hispanic man with a hat scrunched on his head waved at him.

"Good evening, Señor Mayer. I was just about to finish here. I'm sorry I parked in the driveway, but I needed my tools. It was a bigger job trimming the bushes than I thought. I'll work until dark if you want."

He seemed nervous. Aaron was nervous too. Could he carry this off? "Ah, it's okay, go on home. No need to hurry. Finish it tomorrow."

The gardener looked surprised. "You say that but, señor,

you told me . . . I don't want to lose my job."

"It's okay," Aaron replied, "go on home. You won't lose your job."

"Gracias, señor." The gardener bobbed his head and hurried over to the old truck, dragging a rake and a full garbage bag behind him.

Aaron stood there for a moment as the man drove off. He fingered the keys in his pocket and walked toward the front door. He didn't get very far. A man came running out of the house next door, waving at him.

"Mayer! I thought you were going to stand us up again. I'm so glad you made it!"

Aaron stopped and stared at him.

The man was gesturing at him, with harried, wide sweeps of his hand. Aaron tried not to focus on the gardener's handiwork. He'd done a wonderful job. The garden was immaculate. He walked back down the path and over to the neighbor's property. He moved up the garden path, admiring the man's Asian-style Zen garden and the koi pond tucked under an ornamental cherry tree. Even in the encroaching evening light, he could see it had been well tended to avoid leaves and blossoms falling into the pond.

"You usually stomp my garden," the man said, hands on hips. "I . . . wow . . . Well, thanks. I appreciate you walking around."

Aaron tried not to react. Troy stomped his Zen garden?

He shook the man's proffered hand. He'd just figured who the guy was. Nikko Watanabe, a big-time, hot new TV star. He was so sexy with his long hair and form-fitting jeans. Aaron couldn't remember what the name of the show was that the guy was in, but it was an Asian Mafia type thing. *Yakuza.* Yeah, that was it, something about LA Yakuza. He stared at Nikko's hand and realized the fearsome tattoos that graced the actor's body on the show were not his own.

Glancing at the lined-up shoes on a long cedar shelf out the front of the house, Aaron couldn't fail to glimpse the meaningful glance from his host. He kicked off his shoes and left them, facing outward, along with the others.

Nikko Watanabe smiled. "Thank you for that. I appreciate you respecting my religion."

Aaron couldn't speak. The man seemed genuinely grateful . . . almost . . . relieved. He entered the house, stunned by its expensive simplicity. A gigantic Buddha statue lined one wall along with a massive Butsadan. It must have cost a fortune.

Two other men milled around what he assumed was the living room, drinking tea out of an earthen teapot on the coffee table. Aaron hadn't stopped for anything to eat or drink all day and the realization suddenly hit him. He was starving.

"Would you like some tea?" Nikko asked him.

"That would be great, thank you."

"Please, sit." Nikko gave him a little bow and gestured toward a pristine piece of white sectional sofa. Across the coffee table the other two men had stopped talking. They looked faintly goofy balancing tiny teacups in their big hands. Again he was aware of the scrutiny of his broken fingers. He hadn't had the money to get them fixed by a doctor. He'd fashioned his own splints and they were healing well, but his bandaging did leave a lot to be desired. Now he had ready cash he could see a doctor first thing in the morning.

He was about to introduce himself and forced himself to stop. Troy obviously knew these people. He'd have to bluff his way through this meeting.

"It's kukicha tea," Nikko said, handing him a steaming cup. "If you don't like it, please just say so. I'd rather you didn't hurl it across the room like you did last time."

Oh my God . . . is my brother really such a colossal rich prick?

Aaron was aware of his hand shaking a little. "I love kukicha," he said. "It has so many medicinal qualities."

Nikko stared as Aaron sipped. Perfect. He liked the nutty, creamy taste and let the mouthful linger on his tongue. He closed his eyes and swallowed. When he opened them again, he found them all staring at him. The large guy opposite him seemed especially surprised.

"Sorry," Aaron said. He took another sip, worried that Nikko would take the cup from him and send him packing.

"More?" Nikko asked. He glanced over at the other two men as he picked up the teapot. What in the hell was going on? Nikko poured him a little more tea, setting the pot down again then sat to Aaron's left on a decorative looking, rather than functional, chair.

"Well," the large man said, clearing his throat. "First of all, I'd like to thank you for coming here and secondly . . . well, of course we'd like to talk about the tree. I know you've stated your feelings about it, quite . . . *stridently*, but before we go so far as enacting the Tree Act, we'd like to remind you that the walnut tree is ninety-four years old and we'd like to preserve it—"

"Of course," Aaron said, wondering if it would be rude to ask for more tea. He caught Nikko's swiveled glance and looked back at him. Nikko's gaze flicked back to Aaron's now-empty cup and he picked up the pot again.

The large man was blinking. Aaron had clearly disarmed him by his response. That much was obvious.

"You . . . agree?" The large man licked his lips. This was clearly an emotional issue for him. "Wow. As you know, it does lean over and drop leaves and—"

"I'm sorry," Aaron said. "Please tell me what you'd like me to do."

The room fell silent. Nikko kept staring at him, the teapot tipping a little in his hands.

Across from Aaron, the large man visibly relaxed. "That's a shocker. I took a petition around the street and everyone signed it to stop you from continuing to poison it."

Poison it? The fresh cup of tea almost scalded Aaron's lips.

"I would never do that."

"Well . . ." the man cleared his throat, "Your neighbors across the road videotaped you pouring something onto the leaves, throwing it from your window."

Aaron almost choked on his tea. "There's a misunderstanding here. I have no intention of destroying or removing the tree." *Boy . . . my brother tried to kill a tree?*

"Really?" the man beside the large man with the apparently dry lips spoke for the first time. "I was hoping this was the case. We had the tree analyzed and it's hard to tell if the damage to it came from the caustic substance you threw on it, or if it's walnut blight."

He shoved a set of photos across the table at Aaron who set his cup down reluctantly and picked up the photos. He studied the black splotches on the leaves. The lack of the warm cup against his fingers seemed to leave him shivering. His fingers throbbed. He did his best to ignore the pain.

"That's walnut blight," he said.

Again, surprised looks ran between the other three men.

"That's what the tree expert said." The large man shrugged. "The other walnut trees in the neighborhood have it, too."

"I can fix that," Aaron said. "In a couple of weeks, they'll be looking like new."

The three men looked dumfounded.

"Can we have that in writing?" the third man asked.

"Sure." Aaron nodded. "Whatever you like."

"I'm surprised you know about all this. You've been so . . . negative about the tree. Incidentally, how *do* you fix walnut blight?" Nikko asked.

"Oh, lots of ways, but I prefer a natural approach. I'd need to study it more, but it looks like the soil's pH balance is off.

I'd use a Bordeaux mix, burn off the affected areas and — " he whipped through the pictures in his good hand, "I'd want to prune them a little to ensure proper aeration. Blight thrives in moisture."

"My God . . . that's almost exactly what the tree doctor said." The large man sat staring at some pages in his hand. "Why didn't you say something before I spent two-thousand dollars on his expert opinion?"

Without thinking, Aaron leaned across the table and held out his hand.

"Let me pay for the quote."

The man handed over the pages. Aaron glanced at the name at the top of the first page. William Gelt. The name seemed familiar. Why?

"This went better than I expected," Nikko said, jumping to his feet as the other men stood. Aaron understood the meeting was over and held his hand out to all three men to shake.

"I'm sorry for the misunderstanding," he said. "I am sorry about the tree. I'll take care of it first thing tomorrow."

He shuffled out the door aware of total silence behind him. Nikko came outside just as Aaron finished slipping his shoes on again out front.

"Has something happened to you?" Nikko asked.

Aaron froze. "No. Why?"

"Your fingers. They're bleeding."

"Oh, my God. Did I get blood in your house?"

Nikko shook his head. "No, no. I'm worried about your hand. Did you hurt yourself?"

"I slammed them in the car door."

"Doctor Gelt thinks you should go to the hospital and get them seen to."

"But — "

"Do it. Please. Here's his card. I'm so pleased all this worked out." Nikko smiled in the semi-darkness. "I told them all your super-jerk routine was all an act. By the way, per your request, I'm letting you know I will be conducting an early morning prayer service here."

Nikko looked nervous again. The words were weighted, but why? Obviously, Troy had cared what the actor did in the privacy of his home but . . . *why does Nikko think I need to know?* He began to wonder if the man was gay or straight. Had he and Troy once had something that had gone horribly awry?

"Okay," he said aloud. "Have . . . fun." *Have fun? Jesus, Aaron, could you be a bit lamer?* He gave Nikko what he thought was a friendly smile. Nikko looked shocked but said nothing as Aaron hurried down the path.

Next door, he tried several keys until he found the right one, looking around to make sure no one was observing him. Nikko had vanished. It would look so damned foolish for Aaron not to know his own damned door key.

When he opened the door, he could smell lemon furniture polish and—was it sandalwood?—as a young Hispanic woman rushed forward.

"Señor Mayer? I'm sorry. I just heard you come in. So sorry." She looked frantic.

"Couldn't find my key. I . . . I . . . had too much in my pocket."

"But you never unlock it yourself. I'm so sorry." She stared helplessly at him. "I wasn't sure if you'd be home for supper. I just put it in the oven to keep it warm." Her hand shook as she slipped on a sweater. He reached over and helped her with her sleeve.

She seemed surprised but covered the awkward moment with staccato words. "You have several messages. One from Señor Alvarez. He tried to reach you on your cell phone but you weren't picking up, so you should call your message service."

"Oh, okay. Thanks." *Who is Señor Alvarez?*

"Goodnight, señor." She smiled.

"Goodnight." Aaron didn't know her name, but as he watched her hurry across the shiny black and white tiles to the front door, he could tell she couldn't wait to disappear. He stood in the middle of the massive foyer and looked around.

"Wow!" The ceilings were high, and a large chandelier hung in the middle of the entrance hall. Directly ahead was a large spiral staircase, with gold railings, each step carpeted with a deep burgundy material.

The plush rug covered a huge sprawling living room on the right-hand side. Two white leather sofas and a love seat were the only furnishings in the room. Beautiful oil paintings of various landscapes covered the walls. A fully stocked bar and a built-in stereo completed the space. The room was larger than his entire apartment.

To the right was the spiral staircase and straight ahead were several large windows which spanned from wall to ceiling, profiling a beautiful garden, tennis court and heart-shaped pool.

Aaron wandered over to stare outside then glanced to his left. He walked down a long hallway where he found a bathroom. A closet hung open, displaying clean maid uniforms. This was obviously the servant's bathroom. Next door was a large laundry room, and at the back, there was a huge, fully equipped kitchen. Everything gleamed with stainless steel.

Aaron smelled food. Hunger gnawed at him again. He opened the oven and found some sort of casserole. He opened several drawers until he located the cutlery and grabbed a fork. He winced when he banged his injured hand but sucked it up, leaning against the counter. He ate ravenously right out of the baking dish.

It was good. Spicy and delicious. He placed the leftovers in the heavily stocked refrigerator and slowly walked up the stairs. *Who was the man who'd left him the message? Where was Troy's cell phone?*

His fingers throbbed with increasing heat. He glanced down at the oozing bandages. What in hell had he done to himself? He took a deep breath, holding on to his injured hand. He was torn between helping himself and drinking in his new surroundings. The hallway was lined with the same luxurious burgundy carpet. He savored the feel of it as he investigated each tastefully decorated room. Some had their own bathrooms. At the end of the hall was the master bedroom.

When he opened the door, his mouth formed into an unconscious *o*. A round king-sized bed sat in the middle of the room. A walk-in closet stood open, filled with clothes. Off to the side, overlooking the garden, was an exercise room and a luxurious bathroom complete with hot tub and sauna.

"Brother, you know how to live." As he said it, he felt a certain amount of sadness. Troy said he'd be gone, and although he didn't know him very well, Aaron felt a certain emptiness, and confusion.

"This is what you lived, brother, and you wanted out?"

This made no sense. Still a smile came to his lips. He couldn't believe that all this now was his. He jumped on the bed and stretched out. This seemed like a fairytale. Yesterday, he wasn't anybody, someone who lived in poverty, and was in danger of losing life and limb. Now here he was, walking in the shoes of his brother, who had had everything. Why had Troy done this? Why had he let him step into his shoes? Did his brother feel guilty? Did he really think that it was Aaron's turn?

In the master bathroom he undid his bandages and almost fainted. When the loan sharks had come after him, they'd let him choose which hand they'd damage. He'd chosen the left. It had hurt like hell when they took the hammer to his fingers, but he'd gone to the public library and learned about setting them. He'd taped the left middle and index fingers together, supporting them with a homemade splint. How in the world had he hurt them again? He'd thought they were getting better.

He saw beneath the hand wraps a deep gash across the knuckle of the middle finger, which was now swollen. He could see down to the bone. He felt suddenly dizzy.

He had no choice. And he had the money. He picked up his wallet and keys, walked out of his house and went to the hospital.

CHAPTER THREE

He should have been pleased that the car was able to direct him to Cedars-Sinai Medical Center. He should have been thrilled that he didn't need to count the minutes he spent in the parking lot. He had the means to park, probably for the rest of his life.

And, he should have been giddy over getting preferential treatment thanks to his top-notch health insurance. The orderly who wheeled him into the emergency room assured him it was because he was bleeding, but Aaron had glimpsed the human tide waiting for help. Plenty of them were bleeding, too.

They sedated him with Valium, and he drifted in and out of consciousness as they reset his fingers and stitched his wound.

He had odd dreams of butterflies and bears and remembered in his sleep that he'd cut his hand getting on the bus after his night hiding in the woods. That had been the lowest point of his life.

When he finally awoke and lay in a curtained-off cubicle, he was surprised to see William Gelt standing over him.

"I told you I'd help you. Can you sit?"

Aaron's head swooned as he tried. William helped him on with his clothes, keeping up a non-stop patter.

"They found my business card in your pocket and called me. I had no idea you'd broken your fingers. One is almost healed, the middle finger's in bad shape, with that fresh cut. A couple of weeks and you'll be good as new. Can you stand?"

Aaron still hadn't said anything. He felt as if he were walking under water.

"My car," he said after they'd walked out of the hospital to a waiting limousine out front. *A limo? Really?* He couldn't believe it.

"Get Gustavo to bring you here in the morning and you can pick it up. They won't let you drive because of the sedatives they gave you."

They got into the back of the limo. Aaron noticed the peaked cap of the driver, glanced down at his hand, which now had a neat, unobtrusive, soft black cast on the two fingers, a strap around his wrist disappearing under his shirt.

Gelt kept talking. "I picked you up since I figured you didn't want to spend another ten thousand dollars on an overnight hospital stay. They say you need to change the dressing tomorrow. I can do that . . ."

Aaron wondered why the man was being nice to him. He kept zoning out then coming back to the conversation.

"I had a couple glasses of wine, so I didn't want to drive. Tony here offered to pick you up. Even though you punched him in the face last week."

"Sorry . . . thank you."

Aaron was out of it. The man wouldn't shut up. What did Gelt want from him? Was this about the damned tree? He dozed the rest of the way home and was aware of being helped to his house. He thanked the two men, letting them fumble for his keys until they found the right one.

He stumbled into darkness. The hall lights came on as his hand hovered by the wall switch, and he waved Gelt and the driver goodbye.

After locking the front door, he took the stairs slowly up to his bedroom. Shower. He needed a long, hot shower. He took one, keeping his newly adorned hand out of the line of the water spray. Feeling revived, he came out of the fog of sedation and felt merely calm as he toweled off and threw on a pair of sweatpants from the generous selection in Troy's closet.

Now he felt better. His fingers ached but didn't throb. They were bearable. He padded into the bedroom again.

Aaron wasn't sure if he was supposed to feel this sense of entitlement, but he did. Like Troy had written in his letter, it could have been either one of them their father had taken with him. So why did he feel guilty? Why did he feel like he was profiting from what obviously was his brothers' suicide?

He closed his eyes a minute. *Don't feel guilty. You have the right and if you don't do this, all this will go to someone else.* God, if he was even going to carry this off, he needed to study Troy's agenda. Aaron stared at the phone. He needed to know all he could about Troy's life. No one could know. He'd start by finding out about this Señor Alvarez.

He reached over and picked up the phone. A little card beside the phone said, dial 548 for message service. He dialed and waited. "Yes, Mr. Mayer," a voice replied.

"I have a message?"

"Yes, from Señor Alvarez. Would you like to hear the message now?"

"Yes, please."

"Hold the line."

A few moments later, he heard a voice, deep, and low. The man sounded half asleep. "Hello Troy. I'm afraid we're going to have to put off that discussion for a few days. My client is stuck here in London and he needs me to stay with him. I should be home end of the week at the latest. And no, there's nothing you can say to change my mind. We'll talk when I get home. See you soon."

Aaron narrowed his eyes. "Change your mind about what?" he said aloud then hung up. He'd said home, like he lived here with Troy. God, did Troy have a live-in lover? Shit. This complicated things. A lot.

He had no idea if Troy was gay. Aaron got off the bed. If

he'd felt any trepidation before, it was now amplified three times. *Okay, don't panic.* It looked like there was trouble in paradise. *Oh God, is that why Troy did it?* This guy was planning on leaving him? Well, at least he wouldn't be expected to sleep with the guy.

Aaron had had only one sexual encounter with a guy. It was in high school and he and a few friends got loaded and dared each other to give each other blow jobs. When they'd sobered up, no one talked about it. It was taboo, and embarrassing. Aaron could hardly remember it.

He'd had a few girlfriends, none of them lasting more than a month or two. He'd been so preoccupied with his mother, he'd rarely thought about romance . . . but Troy, gay, and living with a man? That blew his mind.

Aaron took a second look at Troy's agenda. Aaron was relieved to see how detailed it was, as if he was giving Aaron a travel book to his life. In the margin were notes like, *long-time friend, business associate, board member, lawyer, banker.*

In the drawer of the night table, he found Troy's cell phone and a small photo album. On the cover of the album, Troy had drawn a heart. Below the heart was written *Dave.*

Aaron felt a little strange opening the album, as if he was delving into the intimate details of his brother's life. On the first page was a picture of Troy with a man, he had to admit, an exceptionally good-looking man. His dark hair, and eyes, along with the golden skin told Aaron he was of Latin descent, perhaps Spanish or Italian. He was smiling, standing on a white sandy beach with a pair of blue swimming trunks on. He was definitely a gym freak because he had great definition in his arms and pectorals. His abs were incredible. And he was tall. His brother, at a good height of five-twelve, came to his shoulder.

Troy was hugging him. They were both smiling, blue sky overhead. Underneath, it read, 'Dave and I in Jamaica, 2010.'

Aaron turned the page. Another picture of Dave, this time

he was standing outside some monument. There was a familiar face standing with him, a rock star, whose name escaped him. The caption read, *Dave on the job, Moscow.* On the job doing what?

A few pages later, and his questions were answered. Personal notes from various celebrities in the form of postcards littered the pages. *Thanks for keeping me in shape. Best personal trainer in the world. Couldn't do without you, buddy, see you next tour.*

More pictures of Troy with Dave, some of them at Christmas, with other people, at parties, fancy dinners. The last one caused him to pause. He studied it for a moment. Troy and Dave were dressed in suits, holding champagne glasses. Aaron couldn't help but notice the gold bands on their ring fingers. "Oh shit. They're married! Fucking shit!"

Aaron almost dropped the album. Troy had been married to a man, a gorgeous, successful man, who apparently was coming home to ask for a divorce. He couldn't let that happen. Not now. He could lose everything. If they had to go to court, it might be discovered that he wasn't Troy. Where did this marriage take place? Was it written down somewhere that they would split everything or . . . *Shit.*

A little while later, Aaron crawled back up on the bed and laid his head on the pillow. He eventually fell off to sleep, his head spinning with information. But he felt safe for the first time. And that was something too precious to give up.

His alarm went off at five am and almost gave him a heart attack. Opera boomed from the sound system. He fumbled with the light then finally unplugged the sound system to shut it up. The music had been loud enough to wake the dead.

He sat up in the bed and glanced around. He'd had a restless few hours' sleep, judging by the disarray of his bedding. He remembered the stuff about Dave. Shit. He was married!

He was either about to experience a total catastrophe or total bliss.

Aaron couldn't sleep so he padded downstairs, made some tea and glanced outside the kitchen window at the walnut tree. The sky was a pale, black-pearl color. Probably nobody else around him was awake. He wanted to get a look at the tree. He retrieved the paperwork that Gelt had given him.

When he read his notes, he saw to his surprise that the tree was Gelt's and that he lived next door. The tree had obviously been the subject of a vicious war between neighbors. Watanabe had mediated. But why? He didn't seem to like Troy much, either.

Aaron found a sweater and some tennis shoes and went outside. He could see the damage from the acid, and yes, it did look like acid had been thrown on the tree, but she was a beauty. He found a shed in his own back yard with trimming tools, a ladder and began tidying up the tree. He filled two garbage bags before carting them around the side of the house where he found his garbage bins.

Two neighbors from across the road were watching him. One of them had a camcorder in hand. Well, he'd done nothing wrong. He heard a truck and glanced out to see the gardener from the day before. This must be Gustavo.

"Hola, Señor Mayer." Gustavo leapt from the vehicle and came to him. He frowned when he saw the garbage bags in Aaron's hands.

Aaron dropped the bags into the bins, aware of the two women across the road watching him. *Man, it really is like Wisteria Lane . . .*

"I want to show you something." Aaron gestured to Gustavo who followed him to the other side of the house. Gustavo stopped and stared at the tree and jabbed a finger. "Who?"

"I did. Tell me, what do you think about changing the soil around the base of it?"

Gustavo's brows flew up into his hairline. "I suggested this to you. You told me to go fuck myself."

Oh my God, my brother is such an ass.

"I'm so sorry. Well, I think it's a good idea now."

From Watanabe's house, the rhythmic chanting of *Nam myoho renge kyo* wafted out, the sound like water over a stony brook. It was quite relaxing at the break of dawn.

Gustavo got a funny look on his fact but turned his gaze away from Aaron.

What the hell's that about?

"We should get the soil," Aaron said, feeling testy about the constant realization that his brother didn't seem to have a single decent relationship in his life.

Gustavo seemed genuinely amazed that Aaron worked side by side with him in the garden. They were a great team. Although he employed the man, Aaron checked with him before pruning or doing anything. Gustavo seemed fine with everything Aaron wanted to do. Three hours flew by. Aaron wanted to get back inside and focus on researching his new life.

There was, he remembered, a lunch scheduled with someone called Matt.

As he walked around the front of the house, he was surprised to see Nikko Watanabe and the two women across the road all chatting. They stopped when he raised a hand in greeting and stared at him.

What the fuck ever . . .

They all seemed to be conferring again. Watanabe came over to him.

"I have no idea what's going on," he said, standing just outside the perimeter of Aaron's property, "but I for one would like to thank you for not blasting us with your opera music this morning, or turning the hose on my guests."

He gestured to the two women still watching them.

"Mrs. Edie says she thinks you've sustained a head injury."

Aaron stared at him. "No . . . let's just say, I came to my

senses and please tell them I'm really not an asshole."

The look on Watanabe's face told Aaron that he had a long way to go before proving that . . .

Dave sat on the end of the bed in his hotel room and stared at the phone. It was eight o'clock in the morning in LA right now. It was four pm in London and from his hotel room he could see the London Bridge. He was tired but he couldn't sleep. Donovan Regent, the CEO of Regents Investments kept insisting that he accompany him to all the after-meeting parties. "You need to learn how to enjoy yourself, David," he said. "You're young."

Every time Donovan went on a business trip, he took him along, and had done so ever since Donovan's doctor gave him a clean bill of health. "Two years ago, I was a sick man, going the way of my father, aiming for a heart attack at fifty. Now I'm fit, and I owe it all to you, Dave. You're one hell of a personal trainer."

That might be so but while he was here in London, his marriage was falling apart. Dave reached for the phone. *It's over. Accept it.* The problem was, he still loved Troy. In spite of everything Troy had done to drive him away, in spite of his cruelty and arrogance, he was still in love with him. They just couldn't live together anymore.

Before he'd left, Troy had pleaded, begged him for forgiveness. "It's like a broken record, Troy. I'll forgive you, and you'll do it again, and again."

"How in hell do I know what you're doing when you're off with your clients? How do I know you haven't been unfaithful?"

"You don't. You just have to trust me. I would never betray you." He'd had a hard time with the last sentence. "I would never break your heart the way you've broken mine over and over."

Troy had begun to cry. It was rare to see him express that kind of emotion. For a minute, Dave almost went to him, took him into his arms but he warned himself not to be taken in again. He couldn't trust him. Everything was an act. Troy was desperate. He'd do anything now, even pretend to cry. "I love you so much."

That was one thing. Dave had never doubted Troy loved him in his own way. He just really sucked at loving Dave . . . Or anybody for that matter. "I know. But it's not enough."

"I'll see someone. I'll get help."

"We tried that before. You are naturally promiscuous. You're not meant to be with one guy, Troy."

"If you weren't gone so much then maybe I could be . . ."

"There you go, blame me," Dave shook his head. "It's over. I want out. I can't keep feeling like shit all the time, Troy. We'll talk when I get back from London. In the meantime, try to keep it in your pants."

Those were the last words he'd spoken to him. Together four years, married for the last two, and his last words really summed it all up . . . *try and keep it in your pants.*

It was weird how nasty Troy could be and yet guys still wanted him. The neighbors all over St. Cloud Road *hated* Troy. Dave saw a different side to him, but lately, the bad side was getting more aggressive. Troy seemed to enjoy chaos. He seemed to relish inflicting pain. He hadn't always been like that . . . or had he? Dave didn't think so. As far as Dave could tell, things got worse after they married, which was crazy considering that Troy had talked him into it.

Looking back, it was as if Troy had thought that would make him be faithful. Dave had never been hung up on making it legal. They were together because they wanted to be, not because of some stupid contract. Eventually, Troy wore him down. They had gone to Canada with a few close family members and friends. Now it was all a damn mess.

Dave pressed in the numbers. He felt bad about not getting to speak to Troy personally. He let the phone ring a few times and was almost ready to hang up when he heard his voice. "Hello?"

"Did I wake you?"

There was silence.

"Troy? Are you alone?" It was always his first thought.

"Alone? Yeah, ah . . . Dave, right? What's up?"

"You sound strange."

"Is that . . . Dave?"

"Shit, Troy. You don't recognize my voice now?"

"Of course, I'm not awake. Sorry. How are things?"

"You know Donovan."

"Right. Sure. Donovan. How was the ah . . . concert?"

"What concert?"

Silence. "Weren't you, ah . . . going to a concert?"

"No. I went to the opera."

"Oh, yes, right. Sorry. Was it good?"

"It was fine. Look, Troy, I was thinking about the house. Do you want to keep it, or should we sell it?"

"No! I don't want to sell the house. Listen, Dave. Can't we put all this aside and agree to be friends? We could still live here, just . . . you know . . . as roommates. There is plenty of room."

"*Roommates*? Troy, are you high?"

"No. I just don't want to split up . . . at least not totally. It would be a bad idea for both of us."

Dave shook his head. "You are fucking unbelievable. Back to therapy then, is it?"

"If you feel you need to go."

"*Me*? If I feel *I* need to go? Now you're really pissing me off."

"Dave. Listen, all I'm saying is that we don't have to split entirely. It's a big house. We can still live here together."

"You said that already."

"Separate bedrooms."

Dave took the phone away from his ear and stared at it. He clapped it back to his ear, gritting his teeth. "Who are you?"

"I'm . . . you know who I am."

"I moved out of our bedroom a few times and you freaked."

"I did? Oh, well . . . I wasn't ready then, I guess. I've accepted it now. It's over but I think we can be friends and . . . we don't need a courtroom."

Dave wasn't sure what to say. This didn't sound like Troy at all.

"So, promise me, you'll give me time to sort through all this stuff."

"I don't get it."

"Please, Dave. The separate rooms will solve things for a while. I think we need some time apart. I won't bother you anymore."

Silence.

"You still there?"

"I'm going to bed now. My head is spinning."

"Okay. Bye."

Dave put the phone down. Troy had a problem with sex. His problem was, he wanted it all the time. And if Dave wasn't available, any man would do. Three times he'd come home unexpectedly to find Troy in bed with another man. One time, it was the gardener. Dave had fired him in a flash. Then Dr. Gelt's chauffeur . . .

Now, he was suggesting they stay together but sleep in different rooms? That didn't sound like Troy at all! The last time he'd tried to sleep on the sofa, Troy had come into the living room and aggressively attempted to seduce him.

Maybe he's getting his act together? Lord, I miss the man he was . . .

Dave lay down on his hotel room bed, trying not to think about things. Whenever he thought about Troy, it hurt. He lay, ignoring the ringing of the phone beside him.

Fuck him . . . I still love him. And yet, I hate him.

He closed his eyes. A single tear leaked from the corner of his eye, despite his steely determination not to give into anguish anymore.

I'm done with Troy. I am so over him. The bastard . . .

CHAPTER FOUR

Dave awoke after a fitful nap. He was still on the bed, but the room was dark. As usual, Troy dominated his thoughts. He remembered the first time they'd met. He'd been just starting out. Back then his clients had been mostly athletes, fighters mainly because of his elder brother, who ran a boxing gym. After a crazy love affair with a boxer who went back to his wealthy wife, Dave decided to start his own business and make his services available to everyone.

The first one to answer his new ad was Darren Mayer. The guy was a rich importer who was running headlong into a mid-life crisis. He drove a muscle car, touched up the gray hairs at his temple with the kind of unnatural brown shade older men favored, and chased after women half his age. He was a hyper man who demanded perfection, and his domineering personality kept his son Troy completely on edge.

When Dave first saw Troy, he was smitten. Blond with blue eyes, and a killer smile, the guy could talk the birds down out of the trees. Troy made no secret of the fact that he, too, was smitten.

Two weeks after Dave began training with Darren, Troy led Dave straight to his house, and into his bed.

The sex was great. In fact, Dave had never met a guy who liked sex that much. And in the beginning Troy seemed sweet and goodhearted, even if every time Darren called, he jumped to attention.

In spite of some reservations, he fell in love with Troy, and six months later, he moved into the St. Cloud Roadhouse with him. He'd been smitten by the famous neighbors and the ghosts of celebrities past. Clark Gable, Carole Lombard, Mario Lanza, Louis B. Mayer, Robert Taylor, Johnny

Carson . . . so many had lived there. He got a kick out of the fact that porn czar Larry Flynt lived in the house once owned by Sonny Bono.

The first time he caught Troy cheating on him was that very first summer. Dave had gotten his first big contract with a movie star. She was doing a film in Rome and he was expected to fly out there for a few days each week.

When an accident on set delayed production, Dave got to come home. He thought he'd surprise Troy with champagne and flowers. Instead, it was he who got the surprise.

Troy never heard him come in. He was too busy getting fucked. The man was one of Troy's prominent clients, an older man in his fifties. When Dave entered the room, they were in bed, grunting like two wild animals. He wasn't sure how long he stood there before Troy noticed.

Dave had packed and gone to his brothers. Troy had begged forgiveness. Finally after a few weeks of being without Troy, Dave went back. He loved him. He loved him so damn much it hurt, and he shut out all the voices that told him Troy was playing him for a fool.

And then, the unthinkable. It happened again. The second time, Troy denied it, but Dave knew deep down, it was true. The last time, he'd caught him red-handed.

He'd stood by Troy all the way. He tried to get him through his anxiety attacks every time his father would hurt him. Dave never understood their relationship. He tried to abide Troy's shitty mood swings. Sometimes he'd ignore them, other times he'd try to deal with them. He'd endured days when Troy would turn off completely and refuse to talk to him.

Dave had swallowed his aversion when Troy would talk down to people and act with deliberate cruelty. And most of all, he'd put up with his promiscuity, even seeing a counselor with him. When Troy insisted that marriage was the cure, Dave had married him. But it was over now. Somehow the passion and the love he'd felt for Troy had waned. He could finally let go.

Things got worse when Darren remarried. Updated make and model wife number four looked alarmingly like model number three. Troy had pointed out some men stick to buying the same kind of car, but this new marriage really got to him.

I tried to tell him he always wanted his father's approval and that he would never get it. I've told him a million times he's too old for that shit . . .

Now, Troy wanted them to live together like roommates? It didn't make any sense. Maybe it was Troy's way of holding on . . .

The phone beside him rang and he took the call.

"Donovan," he said, unable to hide the tenderness he felt toward his client.

"Hello, love. Can you meet me for a spot of tea? They call it a spot here. No idea why but since you are watching my calories, I figure a spot covers a multitude of creamy sins."

Dave laughed.

"I even Googled tea shops. You'll be pleased to know that unlike book shops, tea is still a bad habit in London."

"Glad to know it. Of course I'll meet you for tea. Where?"

"The Ritz, darling. Others say the Savoy, but I got us a table at the Ritz, so we shall spot in fine style. Meet you there in thirty minutes?"

Dave was thankful to leave the dark thoughts behind as he showered, changed and put on a clean shirt and a tie. He examined his face in the mirror as he donned his suit jacket.

I look like shit. I feel like it too . . . He shook his head, as if he could discard his self-loathing and ugly thoughts on the carpet and leave them for the maid to vacuum. He ran his fingers through his hair and walked out the door, leaving the 'please clean this room' card dangling outside on the handle.

Aaron ate the breakfast of scrambled eggs with fruit on the side that the housekeeper served him. Troy called her his maid. Aaron thought of her as the housekeeper and he gleaned that her name was Manuela, thanks to the check his brother had left for him to give her. Aaron watched her cleaning. She watered the orchids on the kitchen windowsill with great care. She seemed like a nice lady and he felt awful that she seemed so scared of him. Over the meal, he looked over check stubs and business accounts Troy had left for him. Nothing in the man's life was pristine.

Even the black, wrought-iron bars he'd put on all the outside windows out front had been disputed by the Bel Air Homeowners' Association. He'd no idea such a thing existed. They wanted them removed. Troy had written a letter that Aaron was certain was filled with lies, saying he lived in fear of his safety and that was why the bars were there.

Aaron realized the issue was serious and Troy had been given thirty days to comply or else the HOA was taking him to court.

Who in the hell did he call to remove the damned things? Luckily a deeper search of Troy's home office revealed a bill for several thousand dollars from a company called Irongate. Aaron called them. The man on the other end said he would send somebody over that day to remove them.

Good. One problem handled. Now, who in hell was Matt? And where and why were they meeting for lunch? Troy had given him details on everyone but this guy. Terribly inconvenient since lunch was at most three or four hours away.

He went through Troy's checks and was horrified to see how poorly his brother had been paying the housekeeper. He asked her to sit down with him at the kitchen table. It seemed that this was an unusual request and she seemed very uncomfortable.

"How is your family?" he asked.

Her eyes reddened. "Sammy has very bad bronchitis." She bit her lip. "Thank you for asking." She glanced at the wall clock. "I should change the bed sheets."

"The bed sheets are fine."

"But . . . you like them clean, fresh every day."

"They're fine." He tried to use his best, most soothing voice. He wanted to know about the woman, but she wasn't making it easy. The least personal question brought emotion close to the surface. He deduced that she worked forty hours a week for him, with extra pay if she came in weekends. What his brother had paid her was insulting.

He tore up the check and saw the fright in her eyes. She must have thought she was going home empty-handed.

"Do you have a bank account?" he asked her.

"No. They close."

"The bank closed it?"

"Too many bad checks." She gave him a meaningful look but said nothing.

"From . . . me?" *Christ, Troy is such an ass!*

"It's okay. I don't mind." She spread her hands.

"So . . . what? You cash them?"

She nodded. Slowly.

"At a check cashing place?"

Again the slow nod.

"But they charge you a fee."

She glanced away from him, looking stricken. Aaron had never felt such white-hot rage. His brother had a strange sense of humor. He had torn up the check but there were still some there with Troy's signature. He had to practice it.

"I'm going to pay you three times what I've been paying you and you'll get it in cash," he said. The housekeeper's mouth opened, but only a wheezing sound came out.

Aaron kept counting out twenties he'd taken from the boat, into her palm.

"Can you drive me to the hospital?" he asked her. "I left my car there."

"I no drive," she said. "I take the bus."

He insisted she take the rest of the day off and went outside to talk to the gardener who jumped with fright as Aaron approached. He went through the same routine with Alberto, who, it turned out, was Manuela's cousin. Alberto for some reason was being woefully underpaid but had never had a bounced check from Troy.

Hmm . . . the man hates women. Interesting . . .

He tripled Alberto's salary on the spot, paid him in cash then gave him the rest of the day off, asking Alberto if he could take him to the hospital and Manuela home.

It was an awkward drive. The truck was in appalling condition, and yet, Alberto kept apologizing to him.

"Please don't apologize. Thank you for bringing me here." Aaron got out of the truck and walked toward the parking lot. Alberto kept driving. Aaron knew from their work records that he and Manuela lived in East LA. He didn't want to think about how they were living. He was still recuperating from his own hellish ghetto.

Dave met his client in the leafy Palm Court of the Ritz. He both dreaded returning to the US and also Donovan wanting him to stay longer. Tea turned out to be a marvelous affair since the hotel staff kept replenishing the tea sandwiches he and Donovan consumed. He'd never experienced that before. Dave wasn't much of a cake and scone eater so extra sandwiches made him happy.

Music from a piano and harp tinkled in the background.

"Have you given anymore thought to my request?" Donovan asked after sipping his first cup of tea noisily.

"Yes, I have, and you know I can't do anything until I've settled things with Troy."

"Oh . . . Troy." Donovan rolled his eyes. "You won't settle anything with him. You'll go back like a beaten dog because he's the only master you've known."

"Actually, Troy's always been very kind to animals. They are his favorite living things."

"Hmmm . . . . which is why you don't have any pets."

Donovan held his cup out to the waiter for a refill.

"He's never gotten over Mitzi being killed. He still blames himself for her getting off the leash and running across the road. He still can't talk about her without falling to pieces."

"Tsk," said Donovan. "Well, I can't say I'm not disappointed, but I understand. And David?"

David? Oh, boy . . . Donovan means business.

"This time, I hope you dump this little turd for good." He signaled a passing waiter.

"May I request a song from the pianist?"

The waiter bowed. "Certainly, Sir."

"Tell him I want to hear *You Made Me Love You.*" He slipped a couple of two-pound coins into the waiter's gloved hand. He gave a wink to Dave. The color rose in Dave's face as he sipped at his tea. Yeah, it was their private joke, how Troy always twisted him around his little finger. Well . . . not any more . . .

Aaron retrieved Troy's car, paid the forty-dollar parking fee and tried not to think about what he could have done with that kind of cash. He had plenty now . . . He got home in twenty minutes and found the Irongate company truck trying to gain access to the gated community.

Aaron told the gate guard that the truck was there for him. The gate swung open and the truck driver raised his hand in acknowledgment, following him inside. At his house, Aaron left the car out front because he had no idea where the clicker was for the garage. The truck driver parked behind him. The guy got out, clipboard in hand, and followed him around the property.

He was a hot dude. Aaron found himself feeling attracted to the man.

Stop that, you're supposed to be married . . .

He signed the work order and left the man to take care of the window bars. He went inside, took a shower and got dressed. For some reason, he felt as if he couldn't get clean enough in Troy's skin. He told himself that a few hours of gardening had a lot to do with it. And it was. Partly. But the dirt in Troy's garden was cleaner than his brother's handling of his business and personal life. He kept thinking about Dave and the pain in the man's voice.

Aaron had no proof, but he had the weird feeling his brother had killed himself hoping that Aaron could win the love that Troy had desired. Could he convince Dave to stay?

He dried off and found plenty of clothes to choose from, expensive clothes. He ended up choosing designer jeans and a beautiful white silk shirt.

The phone in the bedroom rang. He answered it, hoping it would be Matt.

"That has to be the first contractor you've had on the premises that you haven't invited inside to fuck. You must be slipping."

Aaron was appalled by the words and the surly tone.

"Who is this?"

The voice chuckled. "Tony, of course. Don't know what you're playing at, but your nice routine's gonna wear off and you'll be screaming to get my cock up your ass again."

"Don't bet on it."

Aaron hung up, disgusted with the limo driver. His hands shook. He was clearly obsessed with Troy who must have dumped him. What was wrong with his brother that he couldn't do *anything* right?

Aaron did not want the man calling the house anymore. He

called the operator who gave him the number for his telephone service provider and had the number changed.

"It will take twenty-four hours to take effect," the operator said. Aaron made a note of the new number to make sure he gave it to Dave.

Outside, the window bars were down. "I've filled the holes with putty, but they'll need to be painted over," the truck driver said.

Aaron thanked him for his time and paid the man with a credit card from Troy's wallet. He decided to drive downtown to the business address Troy had scribbled in his agenda for the day. That was one way to find out who Matt was.

He sat in the driver's seat for a moment then opened the glove compartment. He found a monthly parking pass for a place called Parkview Suites. He also found a piece of paper with several names jotted down. He breathed a sigh of relief when he saw that Troy had written down the name, Matt. Beside it, he'd written, *best friend, school mate, web site designer.*

The car was pre-set for the Pershing Square address. He arrived, pulling into the parking space at Parkview Suites thirty minutes later. The space number and last name synced. He was glad because there were ominous signs posted everywhere warning of immediate towing for illegally parked vehicles. He nodded to the doorman as he walked up the bricked courtyard to the tower office suites.

"Good morning, Mr. Mayer," he said, tipping his hat. He opened the door and Aaron nodded back.

He took the elevator to the tenth floor. The door opened and Aaron walked down the carpeted hallway. He didn't realize he was going the wrong way until he heard a voice call out behind him, "Troy!"

He turned, looked. There was a guy poking his head out of a door behind him.

"What are you doing, stupid? You drunk?"

Aaron laughed. "Ah, no, deep in thought."

"Missing Dave. Can't say I blame you. When's the hunk coming home?" The guy opened the door and Aaron walked in. He saw the name, Matt Lincoln on the door. So this was the famous Matt. *Nice place. He must do well.*

"Yeah, well. You know."

It seemed natural for Matt to talk about another guy like that.

"What do you mean, you know?" Matt looked puzzled as he walked Aaron out again into a huge room where several large computer systems were scattered. "You can't get enough of his big cock. Can't say I blame you. A million guys would go for that if you let him off his leash. You hear from him last night?"

"Yeah." Aaron cleared his throat. "He's ah . . . fine."

"You're still not thinking of splitting up, are you?" Matt narrowed his eyes.

"It's a little rocky right now."

"You promised to be faithful. I don't get you man, a stud like that in your bed and you screw around! You love the guy, Troy. You'll lose him. Don't be stupid. He's the best thing that ever happened to you."

Aaron nodded.

"Here." He walked over and poured coffee into a cup from the Keurig machine on the windowsill. "Have some."

Aaron took it. "I don't drink coffee."

"Are you nuts? You must drink ten cups a day."

"Matt . . . Yeah, I mean, I'm trying to cut down."

"Whaddya mean, *Matt*? Jesus, Troy, what the hell's up with you today? What the fuck is going on?"

Aaron felt his face growing hot.

"Well?" the man asked, and Aaron took a deep breath.

CHAPTER FIVE

Before Aaron could think up a plausible explanation, the man laughed as he poured a second shot of coffee. He handed Aaron a cup, keeping one for himself. Of course, Aaron had to take it.

"Come on, guy. Get real. Are you going into work today?"

Aren't I at work now? Holy shit. Where am I if this isn't my office?

"Ah . . . I don't know. I guess."

"Thought you loved it there when your dad was gone?"

"Yep, I'll go." *Geez . . . I sound like a twit.*

"So what's the new wife like?"

"Don't know her well."

"How long you think he's gonna stay married to this one?"

"No idea. Probably as long as it takes me to finish this coffee." It felt oddly good slamming the father who'd abandoned him and his mother.

The man he'd thought was Matt laughed. "You are so out of it, Troy. Guess what happened last night?"

"What?"

"I finally got up the nerve to speak with the neighbor down the hall."

"What happened?"

"We're meeting for coffee this evening. He's not as hot as Dave but he's pretty hot."

Aaron nodded. "Good luck."

The man turned. "Matt . . . your buddy here is actin' goofier than usual." He jerked his thumb toward Aaron as a man stood from behind the bank of computers in front of them.

Aaron studied Matt. He was a good-looking guy. His short dark hair seemed to be the type to grow unruly with little effort. He listened to the two men bantering and gathered the first guy's name was Patrick.

"Come sit with me," Matt said. Aaron joined him as Patrick left them. "You're really quiet. What's eating you?" Matt sat behind one of the computers and punched the keyboard.

"A lot on my mind, that's all."

"So are we still going to the dinner Saturday night?"

"Um, sure."

"Dave bought the tickets before he left. He gave me two and said, bring a date . . . so . . . maybe I can get . . ."

Aaron lost track of what Matt was saying at that point. He couldn't cope with each new problem. The stress was eating at him. It had dawned on him that he'd have to see his father and the idea was terrifying. Surely Darren Mayer would know he wasn't the real Troy? His thoughts began to skip like stones across the next ripple of water.

He started thinking about Dave coming home. Would Dave be able to tell that he wasn't Troy? Damn. Maybe the guy deserved to know that Troy had possibly committed suicide. Maybe he should tell the authorities. What if Troy's body turned up in the river or something? Everything began to fade in and out. The room began to turn. He could see Matt behind the computer, still talking but his words weren't making much sense.

Aaron stumbled to his feet.

"Are you all right?" Matt asked, looking concerned.

"Sorry I think I need to be somewhere," he said.

Matt followed him out into the hall. "Are you sure you're okay?"

"Yeah, fine."

"Don't forget our lunch."

Aaron nodded, pressed the down button on the elevator and it opened. "Don't worry," he glanced at him, relieved when the doors closed him into his solitude. What in hell was he doing? What in hell was he thinking? Could he really get away with this?

The doors opened on the ground floor and Aaron hurried through the lobby. *Troy could be dead. If so, I'm impersonating a dead man.*

Aaron found his brother's car and unlocked the door. As soon as he got behind the wheel, Troy's cell phone rang. He'd almost forgotten that he'd put it into his pocket before he'd left the house. He stared at the caller ID.

Darren Mayer.

Aaron took a breath. It was his father. He put it to his ear. "Hello."

"Troy? Where the hell are you? Are you running the business, or what?"

"Well . . . yes . . . I . . ."

"Then why the fuck aren't you at the office? I called and Julie said she hadn't seen you in almost three days. What the hell is going on?"

"Isn't someone ah . . . running things?"

"I hope so because you wouldn't fucking know either way, would you? Jesus Christ, Troy! Is Dave still out of town?"

"Yes."

"You go a little nuts whenever he's gone. You should really tend to your sinking ship there, Troy. He's a good man and you're going to lose him. You don't fucking deserve him as far as I'm concerned. He's going to wake up and leave your loser ass. I don't know what he ever saw in you anyway. I always say, take care of the domestic and the rest will take care of itself."

"And you're such a shining example of that, aren't you!" Aaron snapped. As soon as he said it, he regretted it. *Damn.*

"What the hell was that? How dare you talk back to me! You talk to Dave like that, no wonder he's leaving you!"

"He's not . . ." Aaron's voice faltered, "leaving me." *Shit.*

"Get to the office. I need a report on things. That's enough goofing off. I'll be back on the weekend. By the way, you have a new mother."

"Yeah. So I hear. What number is this one? Four, right?"

"Troy! Show some respect. The wedding was last minute. No time to inform anyone, sorry. Nothing fancy."

"That's not what I hear."

There was a significant pause. Aaron began to perspire in his shiny new shirt. He'd heard that his father had remarried, but who had given him the news? And why did he keep baiting the old man?

His father cleared his voice. "Yes, well . . . don't believe everything you read in the paper. We just invited a handful of our closest friends. We'll have dinner, all four of us, if Dave hasn't gotten smart by that time and dumped your ass."

Aaron was going to reply but the phone went dead. *This is my father? Maybe I didn't miss much after all.*

Aaron threw the phone aside. He glanced in the backseat at the folder laying there. He'd forgotten to take it into the house the night before. It said, *Mayer Imports.*

He brought it to the front and checked the address. Inside, was a press release. Across the bottom were written the words: *Located in the Textile Section of the Historic Fashion District.*

He knew nothing about imports or this historic fashion district, but he guessed he was going to have to learn in a hurry. He punched in the address on East Olympic Boulevard, put the car into drive and slipped into the flow of traffic.

Mayer Imports was a huge sprawling factory on the edge of the textile district, bordering the flower district. He was shocked block by block at how much like New York City the downtown area looked like with its expensive-looking lofts available for rent and for sale. On these same corners, he waited for the lights to change and watched junkies copping crack and smoking right there on the street.

One guy seemed to be having an epileptic fit after ingesting his drugs. His two companions rifled his pockets as he flopped on the ground. Aaron turned the corner and called 911. He reported the incident then kept going, his hands shaking on the wheel. He saw cops and homeless people everywhere.

At the corner of Maple and Olympic, Mayer Imports took up a sizeable chunk of a warehouse building. He had to turn around and as he approached the parking lot, noticed a man sitting in a chair outside the locked lot.

Aaron idled in the driveway. "I'm Aa . . . Troy Mayer," he told the guard.

"No, you're not."

Aaron's heart flipped over in his chest.

The man laughed. "Only kidding, Mr. Mayer. You bin gone so long, we thought you'd been stol'd for body parts." He gave him a big, almost toothless grin and got to his feet, unlocking the gate by hand and pushing it open.

"Thanks," he called out to the guy. He drove into the parking space marked Troy Mayer and sat there for a while. If he was going to screw up, if anyone was going to figure out that he wasn't Troy, this was the place.

He took a big breath and got out of the car. He walked to the main door and noticed there was a buzzer. Beside it was a keypad. He didn't know the code, so he pressed the buzzer, preparing what he'd say to explain it.

"Yes?"

"It's Troy Mayer," he said. "Can you open up?"

"Why didn't you key in the code?" a female voice asked curiously.

"It doesn't seem to work. Perhaps I've mixed it up."

"It hasn't changed since last year. Are you using the old code?"

"Probably."

49

The door buzzed opened. Aaron grabbed it and walked in. There was a long hallway with a variety of offices. A middle-aged blonde woman sat behind a counter in the foyer. "Good morning, Sir. How are you?"

"Hey. Fine and you?" He walked up to the counter and smiled. He had no way of knowing her name.

"I'm good." She smiled.

"I'm sorry about that mix-up outside. What with all the numbers for everything nowadays, I can't keep them all straight."

"Were you using six-seven-eight-zero?"

"Ah, not sure, was that last years? I punched it in so fast."

"The zero is a now a one."

"Ah, okay. So, six-seven-eight-one. Can you jot it down?"

She looked at him. "Your father will freak. You know he doesn't want anyone writing down the codes."

"I know." He laughed, "but just for me. It will be our little secret."

She nodded and handed him a sticky note with the code scrawled on it.

"Thanks."

"Mr. Carson told me to ask you to go and see him the minute you came in."

"Ah, okay. Where is Mr. Carson?"

The receptionist looked up at him. "Excuse me?"

"Where is he?"

"In his office." She laughed. "Where he usually is."

"Okay." Aaron laughed too, then moved down the hallway, hoping to hell people had their names on the doors. He still didn't understand why he had a designated space at Matt's office and oh . . . yeah. There was the lunch date.

At the end of the hallway, he saw a door, marked, *Manager: Joseph Carson.*

Aaron knocked lightly and walked in.

A man in his thirties sat behind a rather messy desk. He

glanced up as Aaron walked in. He was dressed in a blue suit, a matching tie worn loose around his collar. A tuft of golden-brown hair fell over his forehead, accentuating the sharp angles of his face. He got up from the desk, his expression surly.

"Troy! Where the hell have you been?"

Aaron took a wary step back as Joe Carson stampeded toward him. The man slammed the door shut with one hand and grabbed Aaron with another. "I've missed you," he murmured and proceeded to plant a kiss right on his mouth.

Aaron was stunned. He was so shocked he couldn't move. Joe Carson pushed him against the wall and attempted to kiss him again.

"Whoa, wait," Aaron protested, turning his head. He pushed the man back. "What . . . is . . . I mean . . . what are you doing?"

Joe Carson took a step back. "I've missed you. After what you said at the hotel after the conference, I thought that . . ." He trailed off. "I should have guessed. I suppose he's back."

"He?"

"Who else? David."

"Whatever I said at that conference was . . ." Aaron searched for the right words. *Shit. Troy. You were sleeping with the manager? How many other men have you slept with behind Dave's back?* "It was a one-time thing."

Joe Carson stared at him. "A one-time thing? What the hell does that mean? We've been fucking off and on for months, Troy! How can it be a one-time thing? I've already started divorce proceedings. I moved out of the house."

Holy shit!!!

"Oh my God, Joe, Mr. Carson, I mean . . . Joe, I'm *married*."

"Christ, Troy. So am I! You told me that you and Dave were finished."

"Well, I've had second thoughts."

"Second thoughts? I left Jane because of you. Does Dave know about us or not?"

"There is no *us*, Joe."

"Did you tell him?"

"No, I didn't. I doubt he knows. Let's drop it. There's work to be done."

Joe Carson looked upset. *Shit.* Aaron wanted this man to show him the job. "You need to put all this aside," he told Joe. "I want you to take me through the day, show me everything you do."

"What the hell for? You know what I do."

"I'm ah . . . thinking of getting rid of people. Dad wants to increase profit. I may have to justify your job. I want to make sure all bases are covered. I'll do it with everyone."

"We're stretched to the limit now. Your dad made sure of that last summer. And what do you mean you have to justify my job?" Joe's tone turned icy. "I know where all the bodies are buried so just because you've changed your mind about me . . . again, don't think you can kiss me off, Troy."

Aaron felt sweat trickle down between his shoulder blades. The look in this man's eyes made his busted-up fingers twitch. He'd seen that homicidal look before . . . The man who'd come to break his fingers had had the same dead look in his eyes.

"I . . . ah . . . know that but in case, you know. I doubt I'll have to get rid of anyone."

"You're acting strange."

"I'm your boss," Aaron snapped. "Just do it. Let's get started."

Joe looked like Aaron had slapped him.

"Is there anything I should know . . . any recent events I need to take care of?"

Joe gave him an incredulous look. "That shipment of broken vases from Japan is still under review. The company doesn't want to reimburse. You should probably handle that yourself. I'm not getting anywhere. Your Japanese is fluent.

Mine is non-existent."

I speak Japanese? "Okay."

"And Gloria has given her resignation in Billing and Invoicing."

"Why?"

"You know why, Troy, the sexual harassment thing, the incident your dad dismissed. And you told her to either shut up or leave. So she's leaving. It's a wonder she didn't take it to court. Anyway, it's official. She's the one with the most experience, damn good worker. We'll have a series of temps for a while. I put in a call to the agency. It will be a pain. We'll never find another Gloria Gilroy."

"Maybe I can talk to her." Aaron opened the door and walked out into the hallway.

"You did, you told her . . ."

"Maybe I was wrong."

Joe stared at him.

"Who did she accuse?"

Joe followed him into the hallway. "Where have you been? It's like you've fallen through a rabbit hole or something."

"Refresh my memory. I've had a lot on my plate recently."

"Paolo Santini, the guy who works in packing. You understand now?" He gave Aaron a meaningful look. "We can't fire him."

"Point him out when we get there."

Joe narrowed his eyes. "You've forgotten what he looks like?"

"No, of course not, I . . . well . . . just let me know where he is."

Joe Carson fell silent as they walked down the long hallway. It was obvious he was hurt, and Aaron felt like a total shit, but hell, the guy couldn't leave his damned wife for him. *Tough love. I have to be an asshole right now.*

Aaron let him take the lead. He knew the guy thought he'd lost his mind. Things he should know, he didn't. *Fuck. This has been a terrible mistake.* If he couldn't convince this guy, how was he going to convince his own father?

At the end of the hall, Joe reached out a hand and placed it on Aaron's shoulder. "Troy," he said in a hushed voice, "Don't be too hasty about ending this. The sex has been fantastic. What Dave doesn't know . . . you know, can't hurt him, right?"

"It can and does hurt him. I'm really sorry, Joe, but I love him. I have to . . . to make it work."

Joe snatched back his hand as if he'd received an electric shock. He blew out a breath.

"Well, what I'm saying is if you need some more time to leave him, I can be patient."

Aaron simply nodded, not wanting to get back into this discussion. He didn't want to upset Joe any more than he had. What in hell had been wrong with Troy, having an affair at work, with a married man, and he himself married? It explained a lot.

Chapter Six

A fternoon tea turned out to be a lot more productive than
Dave expected. He picked up two new clients who lived
in Bel Air, all because he'd passed the sugar bowl to the two
women at the table beside him. Donovan had been enter-
tained initially to encounter strangers from home, but then
became increasingly sullen. He was as bad as Troy about
needing constant attention and endless reassurance.

One of the women lived a few streets over from the house
he shared with Troy and she told Dave she had a private yoga
studio.

She was of an indeterminable age he guessed was due to
excessive and rather bad plastic surgery.

"My husband had the studio built for me. It has a spectacular view of the Santa Monica Mountains." She scrolled
through her cell phone and showed him photos. She wasn't
kidding. It was his dream yoga studio. He'd asked Troy so
many times if he could build a studio on the property. Troy
had pooh-poohed it. He envied the woman who prattled on
about how she and her friends would pay him individually to
teach classes there every morning. If she was telling him the
truth, by his calculations, he could make an extra thousand
dollars a week teaching the proposed early morning class.

They shook hands on the deal and exchanged numbers.
The woman handed him her card. Stacey Adler. He tried to
place her last name. She must have guessed this because she
said, "My husband, Cliff, is the chief financial officer of Sony
Pictures."

He nodded. It was only one of the biggest studios in the
movie business.

"We'll start Saturday morning," she said.

That gave him two days to get home. Donovan shrugged.

"As long as I still get my private sessions with you, I'm good."

"Thank you," Dave said, squeezing his hand. He wasn't sure he was ready to face Troy yet. Whatever happened, he'd deal with it. He just hoped he didn't find the man he'd married in bed with yet another asshole . . .

The next few hours were tough, but Aaron managed to get through them. He spoke to people he pretended to know and tried to learn a whole business in one day. He was unsuccessful in getting the company in Japan to pay for the broken merchandise. He simply did not speak the language and knew no way around this sticky problem. The woman had been quite haughty. Evidently, she'd dealt with Troy in the past.

How weird. This woman seemed to like the guy . . . now, probably, not so much. It had been hard to explain his sudden inability to speak Japanese to her and his few efforts using Google Translator were a disaster.

Around one-fifteen, he got a phone call from Matt.

"You're really something, Troy."

Dead silence. He had a feeling this wasn't a good something, but a bad something.

"You stood us up. I didn't think you'd do this after what happened the last time."

"Shit, Matt. I'm sorry. The you-know-what hit the fan the second I got here. Can I still meet you?"

"Yeah, if you explain the cast on your hand, and you pick up the tab. We're over at Philippe the Original and we're next in line. We'll order and pay for everything and you can reimburse me."

"Okay."

Out in the hallway, he encountered the secretary to whom

he'd spoken when he first arrived.

"How do I get to Philippe the Original from here?"

She smiled. "You're really going fancy, huh?" Before he could respond, she said, "I'd take a taxi. There's a bunch of them across the road since its flower day and all the Japanese tourists are out in force."

"Thanks."

"No problem." She returned to her task at hand and he ran outside. He grabbed the first taxi he saw at the rank and they made the mad dash across downtown in twelve minutes. He was shocked at what a dump Philippe the Original was. He was even more stunned by how packed it was.

Matt stood, waving at him across the restaurant. Aaron threaded his way over there, pleased to see the man. He liked Matt. They exchanged smiles.

"You owe me twenty-two dollars," Matt said. Aaron was surprised the guy was pushing this money thing then began to wonder if Troy had been cheap with him, just like he'd been with his employees.

"Troy, this is Walter Berman." As the two men shook hands, Aaron apologized for being late.

"Got caught up with some paperwork and forgot the time. I'm really sorry."

They all sat down on one of the long wooden benches shared by multiple diners. Everybody was in business suits and the cacophony of chatter was deafening. Matt slid a plastic red basket toward Aaron. "Dude, here's your French dip."

Aaron stared at the cholesterol in a bucket, realized he was hungry and dipped the roast beef sandwich into the steamy dark liquid in front of him. Fuck. It was amazing. He took a couple more bites.

"You're on good behavior," Matt observed. Now what in hell was that supposed to mean? The three men ate and drank their bottled water and Walter Berman began to talk.

"I think your idea for the global media company is excellent. Balancing the idea of bringing schools to third world countries for women is a very good idea. It's already been done on a limited scale, of course, but as you know, in Afghanistan, the US government has been helping the war widows, those deemed untouchables, to learn computers.

"Your plan to put these women to use in art, media, language . . . it's brilliant. I like your proposal too, about branching into having them work as interpreters for the government. It's fascinating. I noticed, Troy, that you brought up the issue of Farsi interpreters in Iran. The US military has been actively seeking interpreters, but people are scared. They all think they're going to fly off to exotic, distant lands, meet exciting and wonderful new people and be murdered by them."

He bit into his sandwich, talking as he swallowed. "Recruiting from the source countries is fantastic, because, of course, with your global network warning system, you'll be able to screen all your applicants on the spot."

Matt looked excited. Aaron was so stunned he'd stopped eating.

"You gonna finish that?" Matt asked. Aaron shook his head and pushed his food toward Matt. He couldn't believe Troy had been involved in something as . . . amazing and as dangerous as this. Supporting women in third world countries toward their independence! Where did that fit in with his arrogance?

"Your father still doesn't know, right?" Matt asked.

Aaron shook his head.

"He'll have to find out soon, bud. And you're gonna have to tell Dave. God knows why you haven't told him already, but I don't want him to think we're having an affair. We need to be ready to start in four weeks and I'm sick of pretending we're not business partners."

Aaron finally breathed. Now it all made sense. Poor Troy

must have been falling apart at the seams, unable to cope with his labyrinth of lies. If Aaron could pull this off, he'd be a happy camper. He could quit the business with his father, make his new company grow . . . and maybe work things out with Dave.

First things first, however. He opened his wallet and gave two twenties to Matt. "Thanks for picking up the food."

"I don't have change," Matt said.

"Don't need it. I appreciate your friendship."

Matt stared at him a moment, picked up Aaron's abandoned sandwich, and dipped.

"So," Matt said, a smile playing on his lips. "How'd you hurt your hand?"

"It's a boring story, I assure you."

Matt laughed. "Let me guess. You were screwing some guy and his wife came home. You abseiled from his twenty-third-floor apartment and dangled for a while, hurting your hand."

What in hell?

"Nothing so fancy. Slammed it in the car door."

"Oh . . . Troy." Walter shook his head.

"What?" Aaron asked trying to interpret the guy's tone.

"Nothing . . . I just heard you're given to such elaborate stories. And I must say, I'm glad it doesn't appear to be true. Your apology for being late was simple, but seemed sincere and now, the hand injury. Gentlemen, I think my company is very interested in investing in your business."

It bothered Aaron a lot that he/Troy had such a bad reputation. Back at the office, his annoyance flared when he spoke to the woman who was leaving due to the sexual harassment issue. He believed her, especially after speaking with the arrogant Paolo Santini, who seemed to think he could do whatever he wanted.

"Will you stay if I fire him?" Aaron asked Gloria Gilroy later that day. She was far more valuable than the Santini guy anyway. All he seemed to do was stand around a bunch of boxes and collect an insane amount of money for it. It didn't make much sense.

"Yes, Mr. Mayer," a tearful Gloria told him. "I'll stay if he goes."

"Done," Aaron told her.

"What made you change your mind?"

"I just did," he said. "Go back to work."

The last thing Joe Carson told him before he left was, "Wait until your dad comes back. He's going to raise the roof. You know they're golf buddies."

"Why?" Aaron asked him curiously. "One thing has nothing to do with the other."

"You've changed your tune. You usually do whatever your old man says."

Aaron bristled. "Losing this guy is clearly a good thing for the company." It wasn't easy. Paolo Santini put up a fuss when Aaron called him to the office and told him the news.

"I'll have your ass! You can't do this. You can't do this!"

Aaron had to finally ask the security guard to escort the guy out. Santini hollered, even though he had a big fat check in his hand, and he'd signed a contract promising that he would not sue the company for further wages.

Joe walked into his office soon after and closed the door. "Do you know who you just fired?"

"A no-good slacker by the looks of it."

"Troy, what the hell is wrong with you? You just fired Federico Santini's nephew."

Aaron's jaw dropped. Everyone knew who Federico Santini was. He was one of the biggest mobsters in LA although he lived under the guise of a respectable business name. "What in hell was that guy doing working here?"

"Your dad hired him as a personal favor."

"Are they close, my father and that mobster?"

Joe looked at him. "I thought you knew all this . . . Santini has some interest in this place. Remember a few years back when we almost went bankrupt? Who do you think helped bail us out? We do import and export." He gave him a meaningful look.

Aaron looked at Joe. "Does my father own this company, or not?"

"He owns the company but if you ask me, Santini owns him. Whenever he needs something, let's just say your father doesn't hesitate. Shit, Troy, you act like this is all new."

"No, I . . ." He cleared his throat. "Guess my memory needed a bit of refreshing."

Joe gave him a weird look.

No wonder Troy wanted out of the business with dear Papa. He realized then that Troy had gotten cold feet. He'd been afraid . . . of whom?

When Aaron got home, he felt exhausted. He ate whatever he could find in the fridge that could be nuked. He ignored the messages on the phone and fell into bed.

When he awakened, everything was dark. He sat up, rubbing his eyes. He heard something or someone rummaging around. *Shit.* Had someone broken in?

Slowly he crept across the floor. When he opened the door, he let out a shout. A man was coming up the stairs.

"Jesus, Troy, what's wrong with you?" A deep voice asked from the end of the hallway. "You know you forgot to put on the alarm."

Aaron's mouth fell open. The man walking in his direction was tall and dark haired. He had a flight bag in his hand.

"Dave."

The man stopped in front of him. "What are doing home? You usually go out for drinks with Matt on Friday night."

"Ah, he . . . ah . . . has a date with his neighbor."

Dave brushed past him and walked into the bedroom. He

threw his bag on the bed and began to take things out of it. With the light switched on in the room, Aaron really got a good look at him. Well, his brother had good taste. The guy was drop-dead gorgeous, and even if he wasn't into guys . . . this one would have made him sit up and notice. He was tall and in top shape, all those muscles, no excess fat anywhere, just sleek and smooth like a cat. His thick black hair complemented his smoky dark eyes and his face was angular but classically beautiful like a painting you couldn't stop staring at. He was exceptionally male from head to toe and at the moment, Aaron could feel the chill in the air.

He looked up. "I'll just put these away and make up one of the spare rooms," he said.

"Ah, right. I think that they have been made up anyway." Aaron stood in the corner and watched him put away his things in the drawers.

"Are you hungry?"

"A little," Dave admitted.

"Come downstairs and I'll make you something."

Dave glanced at him. "You'll make something?"

"Sure. Why not?"

"You've never cooked anything in your life."

"I . . . ah . . . well, Manuela left something I think."

"Manuela?"

"Yes, Manuela, the housekeeper."

"I know who she is, Troy. You usually call her the maid. By the way, you had the window bars taken down. The neighbors must be thrilled."

"I suppose so. I've been at work all day. I haven't spoken to anyone. Oh, I spoke to the neighbors about the tree. Alberto and I pruned it and put some great new soil around the base." Aaron stopped speaking. "Why are you looking at me like that?"

"You're blowing my mind right now. You pruned the tree?

The one you've been trying to poison?"

"I didn't try to poison it."

"Come on, sweetie. We all know you did."

Aaron fell silent. "It was stupid of me . . . a mistake. You want to try my cooking or not?"

Dave grinned. "It depends. Are you still asleep?"

"No. I'm fine. Go ahead. I'll be right down. Maybe we can talk."

"Tomorrow okay? Your father called me you know."

"He called you? Why?"

"He wants us to have a party for him and Nancy."

"When?"

"This weekend. He wants us to do it here, invite some friends. We'll have to call Doug and Shirley."

"Right." *Who the hell are Doug and Shirley?* "Can you do that?"

He shrugged. "Sure. Should we tell them Friday?"

Aaron scratched the nape of his neck. "Fine by me. What did my father say to you on the phone?"

"He asked me if we were all right, if I was going to leave you."

"What . . . what did you say?"

Dave came closer. "What did you want me to say? I told him it was none of his business like I usually say. He told me to leave you."

Aaron swallowed. Hard.

"Are you going to?"

"Not this minute. By the way, why's the house phone disconnected?"

"I got us a new number."

"Why?"

"Too many people from the past have it."

"You know something . . . you are freaking me out right now. I've been asking you for months to do this."

63

Dave stepped forward and kissed him. Aaron was so stunned he couldn't move. Dave's tongue moved against his lips, his hands going around Aaron's hips, holding him to his body. Aaron felt the man's growing erection against his belly and liked the feel of Dave's hand curving over his ass.

His ass. Aaron remembered suddenly that all he was wearing was a pair of white boxer briefs. He couldn't believe it when Dave's hand rubbed at his cock through the stretch fabric. Aaron's cock sprang to attention.

Dave broke off this kiss. Aaron almost screamed. *Fuck.* It had been, without question, the best kiss he'd ever had.

"I'm hungry," Dave said, against his mouth. "Feed me."

CHAPTER SEVEN

In the kitchen, Dave opened a bottle of wine as Aaron assembled some eggs, cheese and tomatoes from the fridge. He felt jittery from their kiss . . . no. From the intensity he'd experienced between them. *Can I be gay?*

"I bought this when I was in Paris. Donovan and I tried it at this amazing little vineyard. We loved it. I hope you do."

Dave held a glass to Aaron's lips. Aaron took a sip. It was smooth and buttery. And absolutely delicious. Dave gazed at him, a strange look . . . almost anxiety in his eyes.

"Well, I'm no expert, but I think it's fantastic."

"No expert?" Dave pulled away from him. "You think you're the expert on everything, sweetie."

"How do you stand me?" Aaron beat the eggs, pouring the mixture into a casserole dish.

Dave laughed. "I ask myself that every day."

"I'm sorry," Aaron said sincerely. "I'm trying to be a better man."

Dave said nothing. He stood against the kitchen island, twirling the stem of his wine glass in his fingers. Aaron chose another tack.

"My father seems to like you better than me."

"When it comes down to it, Troy, your father always plays us one against the other. He has no place in our marriage. I told you that from the beginning."

Aaron nodded.

"Good." Dave walked past him. "I'm gonna set up my new bedroom. I'll be back in a few."

Aaron leaned against the counter. This Dave was larger than life. And confused. One minute he was kissing Aaron, the next he was moving into his own room. Aaron wasn't sure what to do with him, or how to talk to him. He couldn't afford any changes right now. He walked to the fridge, looking for salad makings.

He began rinsing, slicing, chopping, dicing. He tossed oil and vinegar into the blender and made his own dressing.

He turned at one point and found Dave standing there staring at him.

"You can cook," the man said.

"Of course I can. Want to eat here?"

Dave shrugged. "Whatever. I need to eat and sleep."

Aaron nodded. He got some utensils and a couple of napkins and set them on the counter.

Dave glanced at them. "Thank you."

Aaron shrugged. "David, I know you want to wait. I need to tell you something." He used oven mitts to pull the frittata out of the oven. The bubbly cheesy smell overtook the kitchen.

"That's amazing." Dave seemed impressed. "Where have you been hiding this talent?"

Aaron laughed. "I don't do it often enough, I know, but I hope you like it."

He served them both a huge chunk and handed the salad tongs to Dave who scooped salad onto his plate, then picked up his fork. "All right. What do you want to tell me?"

"I'm sorry. I don't . . . I've been a shit, it seems. I'm not sure why." He met his gaze. "I've got this great guy right here and yet I have this need to wander."

Dave didn't say anything. He put down the fork, his face pale.

"I have been faithful to you since you left, and I've done some serious soul searching. I don't want to lose you. I wonder why I am so self-destructive. Maybe it's the way I grew up. Maybe it's my father. He doesn't seem to have anything nice to say, and I can't seem to please him."

"You are shooting Dr. Leonard's words at me. I know all this, Troy."

"I promise that if you stay, separate rooms, and all, that I won't sleep with anyone at all. I'll go celibate for a while."

Dave started to laugh.

"What?"

"I think you're fucking serious."

"I *am* serious. And I want to be honest, as honest as I can be. I was having a thing with Joe Carson at work, but it's over."

"Troy, I know about Joe."

"You do?" That shocked him. "Oh, well, anyway, I ended it."

"Are you going to tell Jane too?" He began to eat now, as if Aaron wasn't telling him anything he didn't know.

"I, ah . . . if you want me to." He looked down at the floor. He actually felt embarrassed for his brother.

"And what about Frederico, Sam at the bar, that salesman who sold us the alarm system . . . Gelt's chauffeur, oh, and the terrazzo guy?"

"Jesus," Aaron said almost to himself. "I'm so sorry." Tears sparked his eyes. He looked at Dave. "I'm sorry."

Dave's eyes widened a little. "I think you really mean that."

"I do. It's inexcusable to cheat like that on a man you're supposed to love." He'd said the words almost to himself.

"And do you? Do you love me, Troy?" David met his gaze.

Aaron swallowed. What could he say? He cleared his throat and looked at the floor. "I . . . we shouldn't talk about that. We are . . . it's too late for us, but will you stay, at least let me prove to you I can go without it, then we'll talk about this new arrangement."

"How long do you expect me to sleep alone, Troy?" He met his gaze. "You go on this trip of chastity which I don't believe you can do, and you leave me sleeping alone in an empty bed.

Is this supposed to satisfy me?"

"You can . . . sleep with other men if you want."

"What?" He stood. "You want me to sleep with other men now? Shit, Troy, you go ballistic even when another man so much as looks at me twice! And anyway," he shook his head, "I couldn't do that. I'm still married." He held out his hand then narrowed his eyes. "Where's your wedding band? Wait . . . what happened to your fingers?"

Aaron sucked in some breath. "Ah . . . I slammed them in the car door."

"Is your wedding ring on underneath?"

"No. I went to the hospital last night and they set my fingers . . . gave me stitches. I honestly don't know what I did with it. It must be somewhere. I probably took it off and . . ."

"You never take it off. Shit, Troy," he threw up his hands, "you almost had me. You almost fucking convinced me you were being honest. Now, the ring is gone. Who did you take it off to fuck?"

"No," Troy shook his head, "David, it's around. I just have to look for it. I promise. Trust me."

"That's just the problem, Troy, I can't. I bet your fingers aren't even broken."

Aaron sighed as Dave walked out of the kitchen, leaving half his plate untouched. He didn't take more than a few bites of his food. That didn't go well. Where in the hell was Troy's wedding band? Shit, he'd seen that picture of both of them with their wedding rings on. Why in hell hadn't he thought of it? If he couldn't find it, at least he could have picked up one that looked the same.

Except . . . he had no idea what it really looked like. He'd only glimpsed Dave's ring. What if they'd been engraved?

He donned an apron and washed and dried the dishes. He felt totally demoralized as he climbed the stairs. The place felt so quiet. He held his breath. Had Dave decided to leave after all? When he got up to the top, he caught a glimpse of Dave in the room across the hall. He was in the process of taking off his shirt. Aaron stood there for a moment, catching his breath as the shirt came off. Dave's chest and torso were incredible. It had nothing to do with being straight or gay. One couldn't help but admire that kind of beauty. When Dave reached for the zip on his jeans, Aaron hurried past the door. He dared not stand there.

He went into the bedroom and closed the door. Frantically he searched the bureau, the boxes containing watches and gold chains, but no wedding band. Aaron sank down on the edge of the bed and picked up the photo album again. He turned to that photo where Troy and Dave were in suits. He studied the gold bands, exactly the same, simple bands of gold. Then he noticed the writing below the picture. *This was the happiest day of my life. I had my name engraved inside Dave's ring, and he did the same for me . . . he wrote Dave, yours forever. I will never take it off even in death.*

He knew he wasn't going to find the ring. Wherever his twin was, it was on his finger.

Aaron took the photograph out of the album. Tomorrow, he'd have to find a jeweler.

Dave fought the urge to jump Troy's bones all night. He'd missed the man so much. Troy had surprised him with so many small steps in the right direction. Maybe he'd really broken his fingers like he said. Maybe he had been to the hospital. Who knew with Troy?

He lay in the dark, surprised that Troy never came to him. It so wasn't like him. Dave tossed and turned.

I bet he has another man . . . shit . . . what if it's Matt? They're thick as thieves these days.

He nodded off but jet lag robbed him of quality sleep.

Around four a.m., he got out of bed. Troy's bedroom door

was closed. Was he in there? Dave couldn't resist checking. He quietly opened the door and found his husband sleeping, clutching something in his hand.

Shit. Our wedding photos.

Dave reached out a hand and almost touched Troy.

No, I can't. I'm too raw. Fuck. I can't believe he told me about Joe. He never fesses up to anything!

Downstairs, he was surprised to see that Troy had cleaned up the kitchen.

He never cleans up after himself either.

Dave noticed a pile of papers by the phone and started to go through them. He hated spying on Troy, but the man told him so many lies. It was the only way to discover the truth sometimes.

He saw a bill from Cedars-Sinai and was about to examine it when he noticed some mail in a neat pile beside him. A few bills and one letter addressed to Troy. His name had been hand-written. Just *Troy.*

A jealous rage he'd never known before consumed him. Troy hadn't opened the letter. Damn the man. Now his paramours were dropping love notes by hand?

He turned on the kettle, let it boil and steamed the letter open. He glanced out of the kitchen, but he was still alone.

Dave opened the note and began to read:

Dear Troy,

Thank you for being so open and so agreeable at our meeting last night. I hope your hand is better. Dr. Gelt said he brought you home from the hospital late last night. Two broken fingers and a deep gash? Hope the pain isn't too bad.

Mostly, I want to thank you for not blasting my prayer meeting with loud music this morning. And thank you, too, for not coming out and turning your garden hose on my guests.

Yours,
Nikko Watanabe

Dave stared at the note. He re-read it a couple of times and began to feel awful. Troy had told him the truth about his hand. He'd turned his back on him. He couldn't stand the cold front between them. It made him ache. He sealed the envelope closed, put it back with the rest of the mail and ran up the stairs, thrusting open the door to the room he'd shared with Troy.

He threw himself on the man sleeping in the bed and covered his face with kisses. "I'm sorry, Troy. I didn't believe you."

Troy seemed stunned at first, but soon began to return the kisses. Dave slid Troy's underpants down his legs. He tossed them to the floor. He wanted to fuck Troy so badly, but as soon as Dave attempted to go anywhere near Troy's ass with his fingers, Troy went crazy and tried to struggle away.

"No, not that. You can't do that!"

Dave was shocked. "I know you want to be celibate, but darling, I'm your husband! You love it when I fuck you."

He bent his head to his partner's cock, batting away Troy's hands.

"I . . . not this time, okay?"

Dave looked up at him.

Troy was serious about this celibacy thing. He couldn't believe it. "Do you want me to stop?"

"If you want to . . . you know . . . do what you're doing now, it's okay. I mean . . . I think I like it."

Troy seemed almost shy. It didn't make any sense. Troy was the most uninhibited guy he'd ever known when it came to sex.

Dave smiled faintly. "You think? Okay." He returned his attention to Troy's cock, planting his lips at the base for a moment. He knew his cock so well. But there was something different about it. It had to be his imagination, but it seemed a little bigger. And he'd noticed a few minutes ago that Troy was thinner than he had been, too. "You've lost weight," he said, taking his lips from the crown of Troy's cock.

Troy lay there, looking down at him, his mouth open. His chest heaved. "Not really." Troy's voice sounded strange.

"Yes, really."

"It's probably . . ." Troy began but Dave bent his head again and began to suck his cock. Troy flopped around on the bed, his body reacting to everything Dave did to him. He let out a yell when Dave swallowed his cock to the hilt. "Gaaah!" He shouted when Dave released his cock from his mouth with a pop.

Dave sucked it back in again. Troy's ass rocked from side to side as Dave released him then sucked him back a third time. It was hard keeping up with the slippery eel of a man twisting underneath him on the sheets. He could feel Troy's cock head mushrooming now in his mouth and Dave gripped his husband's hips.

He kept his mouth tight and still. Troy came hard, flooding his throat. Dave kept sucking and Troy kept coming. A strange garbled sound came from deep within his husband's chest and throat.

Man, Troy had never come like this. It just didn't stop. Dave couldn't take it all. He came off Troy's cock, full of apologies, but Troy was in heaven.

"Oh my God," Troy finally spoke. His eyes fluttered open and shut. Dave kept swallowing. "That was incredible, that was . . ." And then . . . the unthinkable. The front door downstairs opened and closed.

A voice from below called up.

"Wakey wakey, boys. Daddy's home!"

CHAPTER EIGHT

Aaron felt as if he was in a dream. The big, booming voice coming from downstairs hacked into his dream like a character out of *The Texas Chain Saw Massacre*. Had this man lying next to him just sucked him to heaven and back? *Jesus Christ*. In high school, it had been fun but . . . this . . . *this* . . . It was an intimacy he'd never known, one that could become an addiction. Now, if this guy would do this for him every night, that would be just fine . . . but there was more to it than that. Dave had wanted to . . . well . . . *fuck* him, and he'd never been fucked before. He didn't think he'd like it. *Damn. What have I gotten myself into here? I am not my brother.*

Dave rolled onto his back and groaned in frustration. "Fucking Christ, Troy! It's Darren. I told you that you should have gotten the key back when you took over the house."

Aaron didn't get the chance to answer. Dave got out of bed and walked over to retrieve a robe which hung on the back of the door. Aaron's eyes widened as he ran his gaze over Dave's naked body. *Beautiful.* He could hardly take it all in, like a marble statue. *Absolute perfection.*

He had the sudden urge to pull Dave back to bed, regretting that he hadn't run his hands over all those muscles when he'd had the opportunity. Didn't mean he was gay, he thought, as he watched Dave slide on a white terrycloth robe. He was simply admiring the man like one would admire a work of art. The guy gave a blowjob like there was no tomorrow. It wouldn't be too difficult to touch him . . . or maybe even jerk him off. He wasn't sure about putting Dave's cock in his mouth, though. That was a whole other thing.

The door opened and a tall, well-built man stood there. He glanced around the room. "You boys sleep like the dead or what?"

Aaron pulled the blanket up to his chin, staring at him. He could see some of his own reflection in that face. *My father!* God, this was hardly the reunion with his father he'd envisioned.

Dave scowled at the man who'd invaded the bedroom. Darren Mayer cuffed Dave on the head as if he was a small boy. "Come on, plenty of time for this stuff. Welcome back, son!"

Dave managed a civil smile and straightened his hair with a shaky hand. "You realize what time it is, Darren?"

"Early bird gets the worm, kid!" He walked over to the bed and looked at Aaron. "You and I got some talking to do."

"Could I get dressed first please?"

"I don't like your tone," Darren Mayer replied.

"Darren!" Dave interrupted. "Please wait downstairs. I'm sure the coffee has been made. Troy will be down shortly."

Darren Mayer sighed and walked to the door. He cast a glance at Aaron that felt like little steak knives. "Now that you're back, David, maybe Troy will come to his senses." The door closed behind him.

Aaron was in a state of shock. His father, the father he couldn't even remember, had just marched right into his bedroom and bellowed at him like he was a slave.

Dave glanced over at him as he belted his robe. "That's the last time your father does that. If you don't stand up to him, Troy, I will."

"He crossed the line," Aaron said. "I'll deal with it."

Dave came closer. "Really?"

"You seem surprised. I'm twenty-seven-years old. He treats me like a child."

"What's happened to you?"

"What do you mean?" Aaron got out of bed, wrapping himself in the blanket.

"Like this. You and the blanket . . . you're so modest all of a sudden, as if I haven't seen you naked a billion times."

Aaron felt himself blush. "Well . . . I'm having a modest day, that's all."

"And you're really going to stand up to your father? Because usually you don't say boo."

My God. Was Troy really that scared of the man?

"I'm going to take a shower," Dave muttered on his way out of the room. "If you haven't taken care of it by the time I come downstairs, I'm going to this time. I mean it."

Aaron sighed. He pulled on some jeans and a sweatshirt, ran his fingers through his hair and padded downstairs in his bare feet. The man who'd given life to him stood outside by the pool, a mug in his hand. Aaron slid open the patio door.

Darren met his gaze. "What in the fuck are you trying to do, ruin me? You fired Frederico Santini's nephew!"

"He was a jerk!"

"You had *no* right. Do you know the shit I'm in now? I've had to practically kiss Santini's ass, not to mention his nephew's."

Aaron felt his own temper flare. "Did you hear what I said? Paolo Santini was a jerk. He sexually harassed one of your best employees and —"

"He can do what he wants. He's been hired back, and I've had to promise him a higher salary to boot."

"What the fuck! You can't do that."

"What do you mean, I can't do that? It's my fucking company! I can do what I want, and you'll do what I tell you to."

"We'll lose Gloria Gilroy."

"Fuck Gloria." Darren's agitated gestures sloshed coffee from the mug in his hand. "And about this party you're having for your new mother and me —"

"She's not my mother. My mother is dead!"

"Show some respect. Tiffany is looking forward to having a son. She couldn't have any children."

"Tiffany, I thought her name was Nancy?"

"Tiffany is her stage name."

Aaron rolled his eyes. "A stripper?"

The man in front of him took a step back. "That's no way to talk to your father, boy. Show some respect."

This *show some respect* routine was beginning to wear thin. "I'll be glad to do that when I see some respect coming from you. Which leads me to the next issue. I'd appreciate it if you'd call before you come barging into the house. And I'd like the key back, please. This is my house now."

Darren didn't reply for a moment. Then, he took the key out of his pocket and dropped it on the patio table. "Make preparations for the dinner." He shoved the coffee mug at him. Some of the stone-cold liquid slashed onto Aaron's sweatshirt. "And I'll expect you at the office today to help me clean up some of your mess!"

Aaron clutched the mug to his chest.

The patio door slid open and Darren disappeared into the kitchen. A few minutes later, a car motor sprang to life.

Aaron picked up the key and walked back inside. He discarded the coffee cup in the sink and poured himself a big glass of orange juice.

Dave let the warm water run over him. He closed his eyes, his cock in hand. He was horny as hell. He'd just realized that although he'd gotten Troy off this morning, Troy hadn't so much as touched him. A few kisses, that's all he'd gotten, and even they had been strained at first, as if Troy didn't want his kisses. It had taken him a few minutes to warm up. He didn't understand it. Usually Troy was all over him. Maybe it was this chastity thing.

With his back against the tiles, Dave stroked his cock a little harder, his breathing coming fast. He wanted to come. He needed to come, but he'd always hated to do it alone. He was a man who enjoyed sex, enjoyed the human touch, the anticipation of what his lover would do next. Alone in the shower beating off was not his thing at all.

Finally, he gave up. As he toweled off, he thought about this celibacy thing Troy had proposed. Could Troy really pull it off? Could he go cold turkey without *any* sex at all? If he could do it, maybe it would break this addiction he had to getting laid by every available cock in sight. Maybe Dave could begin to trust him again.

He dried his hair, left the shadow he had going and pulled on some jeans and a white T-shirt. He glanced at himself in the mirror. He was a fool. He'd been a fool for Troy for so long he didn't know how to be anything else. He'd really tried to stop loving him. He'd tried to stop wanting him. He shouldn't have gone to him this morning. Troy would only play him again. No, if Troy really wanted to make this work, he'd have to prove it.

"Let's do it," Dave announced when he walked into the kitchen and found Troy there, leaning against the counter, drinking orange juice.

"Let's do what?" he asked.

"Your test." Dave took down a mug and went to pour some coffee. "No sex for a month, for either one of us."

Troy looked over at him. "O . . . Okay."

"Can you really do it?"

"Sure. That means with each other too, right?"

"Exactly. If you can remain faithful to me with no sex at all, maybe we have a chance." Dave sipped his coffee.

"Worth a try."

Troy's reaction seemed very nonchalant. There was no enthusiasm in his voice. "Are you sure? You sound . . . disinterested now."

"I'm a little distracted." Troy looked at him. "We need to

plan this party."

"Um," Dave said, blowing on his coffee. "I know."

Aaron found his gaze traveling over Dave. His skin was golden bronze and that shadow on his jaw emphasized his masculinity. *Sexy.* Dave was a very sexy man.

Aaron shook himself. What in the hell was wrong with him? The fact that the guy was so damn male in every way should have put him off, but what this guy could do with his mouth was incredible. Somehow all Aaron could think about now was how this morning he'd missed his chance to touch him, to run his fingertips over that bronze skin, to press his lips to those secret places and . . . *damn.*

"Troy?"

"What?" Aaron brought his gaze up to Dave's face.

"Is there something wrong with what I have on?"

"No, you look great. I . . . hey . . ." Aaron took a key out of his pocket and dangled it in front of Dave. "Look."

"What's that?"

"My father gave the key back."

"Your father?"

"Ah, yeah, my father," Aaron replied hesitantly.

"You're calling him your father now? You never call Darren your father. You call him Darren."

"I . . . yeah . . . well . . . he gave the key back so I figured he earned the title today."

"Oh. Well, I'm impressed. "

"And I told him not to come over unannounced anymore either."

"That's what your analyst would call progress."

"Really?" Aaron grinned. "I just call it balls."

Dave gave him a distinctive nod. "That, too!" He turned and rinsed his coffee mug in the sink. "I've got to go into the office."

"Me, too. What do we do for this party thing?"

"You want me to call the caterer?"

"Yeah, would you? And who do we invite?"

Dave narrowed his eyes. "Well, Doug and Shirley for sure, Darren's dearest friends."

"Right."

"Troy, you're the party slut. Usually, you're raring to go when it comes to planning these things. What's gotten into you?"

"I'd like to see what you can do this time." Aaron waited for his reaction.

"Okay," he sighed. "I'll do it. Only fair."

Aaron watched Dave walk out of the kitchen. He closed his eyes. He didn't relish going to that warehouse today. There was too much shit going on there, perhaps shit that Troy had wanted to get away from.

He walked into the living room, watching Dave drive away from the curb in a silver Lamborghini. He couldn't believe that a little while ago, Dave had been in his bed, sucking his cock . . . um . . . like a goddamned champion. What in hell made Troy go elsewhere when he had paradise at home? The thought of it made him horny as hell. It was as if Dave had awoken a sleeping lion.

Aaron ran up the stairs and stripped off his clothes. He needed to shower before he went to the warehouse. He wrapped his damaged hand in plastic and stepped under the spray. As the steamy water ran over him, he closed his eyes and stroked himself. When had he gotten hard? Damn. He knew the answer. He'd gotten an erection the minute Dave had walked into the kitchen. Perhaps it was thinking about all those hard muscles or, yes, he'd definitely caught a glimpse of Dave's cock when he'd gotten out of bed. It was big, daunting . . . intriguing. Could he put that cock into his mouth? Um.

He squeezed a little harder around the shaft. "Yes, yes . . . that's it . . . that's it . . . Dave. Um . . . yeah!"

He let out a shout as the come dripped through his fingers. His eyes closed and he ran a tongue around his lips. *A fantasy.* That's all Dave was, pure fantasy. He wasn't his, not really. It was only pretend and when it was pretend, it was all right.

Aaron got out of the shower, toweled off, his flesh tingling a little. Was he gay? Was that a gay face that looked back at him through the smoky glass? When Dave had made him come this morning, he hadn't felt gay or straight. He had just felt fucking fantastic.

"Well, brother, you left me everything else, why not have that big hunk of yours as well? He's willing, he wants me . . . nothing wrong with letting him suck my cock, is there?"

The face in the mirror didn't answer right away.

"Come on, Bro. What do you say?" he coaxed.

You think a man like that will be satisfied by just sucking your cock? You're going to torture him, not let him fuck you? You don't know what you're missing, Bro!

Aaron took a step back, surprised. He knew he was talking to himself, yet those words seemed to come from deep inside. He had to face it. Dave was not just going to suck him off every night and expect nothing in return.

"Okay, I can touch him, I can jerk him off. I don't have to suck his cock or let him . . . well . . . fuck me, do I?"

He sighed as he got dressed. "Damn it, Troy, did you have to be such a slut? Now, he wants it because you gave it to him all the time."

Aaron knew he couldn't have it the way he wanted. If he wanted to experience the pleasure Dave had given him this morning, he'd have to put out himself. Maybe he could stick to this celibacy thing for a while, or maybe the thought of Dave's mouth on his cock would drive him out of his mind.

Outside the house, he exchanged friendly greetings with his neighbors on both sides and surprised the gate guard by wishing him a good day.

In the car on his way to work, the question played over and over in his mind. *Wonder if it hurts getting fucked?* He wondered if he could take it, a guy's cock in his ass or in his mouth? Dave was pretty big. When he drove into the parking lot of the warehouse, he felt guilty about having made the entire drive on auto pilot.

Damn . . . maybe Troy is in me. Maybe he still has the wheel after all.

He decided he was going to play along with the celibacy thing for a while, gain Dave's trust. Troy had sure as hell done all he could to destroy it. He'd take it one day at a time. He couldn't risk letting Dave go further and then pushing him away. Dave would know something was up. No. He had to be absolutely sure he could be everything to Dave before getting into it.

It was like this place, he had a lot to learn, a lot to experience, and he wasn't that keen on uncovering its mysteries. He had a feeling he'd find a lot of rot if he asked too many questions. *My God, what are my father and brother into? Mobsters!* Aaron thought that *he* was supposed to be the 'troubled' one.

Aaron nodded to people as he walked into the building. This time he plugged in the right code. Joe Carson was in his office as Aaron went by, and immediately he was chasing after him "Slow down, Troy," he said. "Do you know what happened?"

"Yeah, that asshole was hired back, and Gloria quit."

"Your father was really pissed. I told you not to do it."

"Yeah, he's pissed, so what?" Aaron kept walking.

"Is Dave back?"

"Yeah."

"He fuck you good and hard last night?"

Aaron paused. He took a breath. "None of your business."

"Troy, why are you torturing me? I didn't even know I

was . . . you know . . . gay . . . before you. I've given up every-thing. And now it's like all the promises you made. Does Dave know about us?"

"Yeah, apparently he's always known."

That seemed to surprise Joe and took some wind out of his bluster. He looked a bit frantic. "Does he know how you said you loved me, how you said," Joe lowered his voice as a cou-ple of office workers walked past, "how you said you were going to leave him for me?"

"I was an idiot to say that. I'd never leave Dave for you. Now, stop it, Joe." Aaron gave him a little push and kept walking.

"You're going to regret that," he called out.

Aaron swallowed and kept moving. He stopped when he came to the office marked Troy Mayer and slipped inside, closing the door. Maybe he could hide here for the rest of the day, but with his father's office next door, he doubted it.

He sank down into the overstuffed leather chair and looked at the things on Troy's desk. Computer screen, paper weight, a dusty photograph of Dave. He picked it up. Dave was dressed in a beautiful deep purple shirt, standing in front of some fancy hotel.

Aaron studied the image. Did Dave have to be so gor-geous? He put it back down then opened the drawers and started to rifle through things. Most of the papers were ledg-ers concerning accounts, or lists of items which had been im-ported, and their various conditions. There was nothing to give him any clue about the business and its connection to the mafia.

Why did Troy call their father by his first name? It per-plexed him.

He leaned back in the chair his gaze fixed on Dave's pho-tograph. He closed his eyes for a moment, not realizing he'd drifted off until he heard two loud voices in deep discussion.

His eyes flew open and he got out of the chair, creeping closer to the open door. One of the voices belonged to his father. The other one had a heavy Italian accent. Aaron stood perfectly still and listened.

It was obvious that Santini was not happy about something. He referred to some shipment, he said, "millions." In fact, he said "millions" a few times. Then he left rather abruptly. Santini's angry strides shook the walls of Aaron's office as he stormed down the corridor.

Aaron's father didn't come and speak to him again that day although he'd told him earlier, they had a lot to talk about. In fact, Darren Mayer left his office in the early afternoon.

Joe Carson was waiting for him in the parking lot when Aaron walked outside. He groaned inwardly. "Shit," he said between clenched teeth then tried to smile. *What had Troy ever seen in this fool?*

"We need to talk," Joe said, leaning on his Jeep. "I can't sleep, I can't eat. Man, my life is a mess because of you. All I can think about is fucking that tight little ass of yours. Oh, Troy, you love to be fucked so much and . . . let's go somewhere, now." He licked his lips.

"I told you," Aaron said, reaching in his pocket for his key, "it's over. It was what it was and . . ."

Joe Carson reached out and grabbed Aaron by the collar. He shoved him against the car. His face was angry. "You can't treat me like this, Troy, use me and then throw me away. I won't let you."

"Take your fucking hands off me, Joe!"

The security guard came walking out into the parking lot and Joe let go of him abruptly. "This isn't over." He pointed at Aaron then got into his Jeep and roared out of the parking lot. Luckily the security guard had missed the exchange.

"Good evening, Mr. Mayer," the guard called out.

Aaron nodded, trying to smile. He was still shaking. He opened the door of the car and got in. He waved to the guard as he drove slowly off the lot. Shit. Carson meant business. *Troy, damn it, brother, how many people's lives did you play with?*

CHAPTER NINE

Dave regretted offering to get this party together. Even though his personal assistant, Grace, was helping him, it was exhausting. The party was less than a week away, and he still hadn't picked out the menu, or booked the orchestra. There were just too many fiddly little details, and he was swamped with work.

The invitations had gone out, however, but he wasn't sure if he'd included everyone on the list Troy kept in the desk drawer. Troy kept crossing off people and adding new ones in the margins. Mostly they were people Troy had pissed off in some way, and now wanted nothing to do with him. So many names crossed off and scribbled in the margins, he could hardly read them. No. He should have let Troy handle this. He was so much better at it than he was.

At five-thirty Dave was ready to go home. He drove up into the driveway in front of the house, only to see a baby-blue Caddie sitting there. He stopped and got out, narrowing his eyes curiously. *Who was that?*

A heavily made up woman in her twenties was painstakingly making her way down the cobble stone walkway in six-inch stiletto heels. The shoes were blue like the car. She wore a short, rather wispy white dress with a black ribbon in her blonde hair. When she noticed him standing there, her face exploded into a bright smile. "Troy, darling, I knew you'd be absolutely gorgeous."

She made a lunge for him, almost tripping on her heels and Dave opened his arms just in time to catch her. Otherwise, the woman would have fallen flat on her face.

The woman rubbed her hands almost obscenely over the muscles in Dave's arms and purred, "Oh my, my, you are quite the specimen of manhood." She looked up into his face. "I think I've died and gone to heaven. Tell me, darling, I can change your mind about the gay thing."

Dave set her upright on her heels and released her. "I'm not Troy." He gave her a tight smile. "I assume you're Nancy."

"Yes, Nancy. Mrs. Nancy Mayer, in fact." She winked. "Darren prefers Tiffany. It's my stage name."

"I see."

"I came to visit my stepson. I thought we should get acquainted." She reared back and undressed him with her eyes. "I didn't expect him to, oh my." She put her hand to her mouth and giggled rather obscenely. "You're not Troy. You're the personal trainer, Troy's lover."

"I'm his husband, actually. Troy is still at work." He looked around. "I guess."

"Too bad." She grinned. "I mean, well, we could spend a bit of time, you and I." She cupped her breasts and said, "These could use a bit of toning."

Dave cleared his throat. "Yes, well . . . ah . . . feel free to contact my clinic. My receptionist can set you up with a personal trainer."

"But, darling, I want something beautiful to look at while I suffer, and you. Are. Beautiful."

Dave wasn't sure what to do with Nancy or Tiffany. She was Darren's wife. He couldn't be rude to her, yet there was no way he was going inside the house alone with this one. "Why don't we go around back? We can sit outside. I'll fix you a drink."

"Oh, honey." She grabbed his arm. "You just read this poor girl's mind."

Dave walked slowly as Nancy tottered on her shoes at his side. A few minutes later, he had her installed in a lawn chair. She proceeded to lift her dress a little higher than would have been considered decent and gave him a beguiling smile when she knew he had noticed.

Dave slipped inside the house and made Nancy a gin and tonic. As she drank her cocktail and chatted on about the honeymoon Darren had taken her on, he politely stood nearby, listening. He checked his watch every once in a while, and wished Troy would get home.

"Ever go skinny dipping?" she asked out of the blue, batting her big false eyelashes at him.

"Ah, sure. I guess."

"I'm so hot. I feel like a dip. If I strip off, can the neighbors see?"

Oh good Lord. "Yes, they can see. It's not a good idea."

"Sweetie." She kicked off her blue satin pumps and got to her feet. "See these Blahniks? They're my 'something blue' from my wedding. They cost a thousand dollars a pair. What do you think of them?"

Before he could respond, she threw them over her shoulder into the pool. He almost laughed but he was afraid of encouraging her. *Oh, my God, she's a train wreck.*

"The neighbors can see . . ." She narrowed her eyes. "That's the best reason for skinny dipping I've heard. Care to join me, handsome?"

Dave opened his mouth, but no words emerged. The dress came off and then the bra. She stood there in nothing but her skimpy panties. Dave wasn't sure where to look so he glanced toward the kitchen just in time to see Troy at the window, watching them. *Thank heavens!*

Nancy made a running jump into the pool just as Troy got outside. "Who's in the pool?"

"Ah, your new stepmom," David replied. "Nancy, A.K.A. Tiffany, naked or practically naked in the pool."

"She took her clothes off in front of you?"

"Yep, me and the neighbors."

Troy started to laugh. "You should see the look on your face. It's priceless."

"I bet." Dave nodded.

"And her shoes wanted a swim, too, I take it?"

Dave nodded. He wanted to get away from Mommy Dearest. Fast. "Well, since you're here now, I'll leave you two alone . . . to bond."

"Gee, thanks. Just remember," Aaron called as Dave headed to the door, "she's your stepmother-in-law."

"Joy!" He opened the patio door and closed it behind him.

Aaron sat down in the lawn chair and watched the woman as she floated on the water, everything bobbing around. Well, he had to hand it to her, she wasn't modest. He sipped the glass of lemonade he'd poured himself and thought about the conversation he'd overheard today at work.

If he'd understood everything correctly, the company was more in hock to the mob than he'd originally thought. He'd heard 'police.' He'd heard 'containers at the port.' He was pretty sure there were drugs involved somewhere.

The pale blonde woman was swimming over to the side of the pool now. "Hey, Troy," she sang out. "I'm your new mommy."

"Hello, Nancy. You're too young to be my mommy, why don't you just be Nancy, okay?"

She giggled like a girl. "That's right," she said. "We're the same age."

You'd never know it.

She started to get out of the water. She had absolutely no pubic hair. It was kind of creepy. Aaron jumped up and put a towel around her.

"Why, thanks," she purred, "what a gentleman you are. Call me Tiffany if you like."

"I prefer Nancy. Is that okay?"

"No problem."

He sat back down.

"So that big hunk of man you got, he must be something in bed," she drawled as she casually wiped her hair.

Aaron just looked at her.

"Come on, Troy, you can tell me. We're family now. He's got a big cock. I can tell, and he'd be a pleasure to ride. Bet you ride that beauty all night long. I would. Oh my God, honey, you're blushing."

"No, I'm not blushing."

Nancy leaned closer. "You go through a lot of lube, right? It's okay. With a lot of lube, God, it's so good. Your father does it with me that way, up here." She pointed to her ass.

Aaron's eyes widened. Okay, he didn't really want a visual on what she and his father did in bed.

"Hurt the first time but not anymore. I love it that way, the rougher the better, just got to open up a little. And you got to have the right man, and sweetie, that big buck of yours, I'd take him on in a heartbeat. He's the prettiest thing I've ever seen. Do you share?"

"No. You can't have him," he muttered then smiled.

She laughed. "Of course I can't. Don't blame you. I wouldn't share him either but it's a damned shame. Maybe one night at a party when we've all had a drink or two . . . or three, you might let him off the chain for a bit. I'd just love to see him naked."

"Don't count on it." He tightened his mouth. Suddenly he realized he meant it. *Aaron, you have no right to be possessive of him. He's not yours . . . hell . . . you don't even let him fuck you.* He tried to still the voice in his head. No, he couldn't call Dave his, but that didn't mean he had to share.

Nancy rattled on for a bit. She enjoyed talking about sex and her gay male friends and their sex lives. In spite of the fact that she babbled a little aimlessly, there were small bits of information he found interesting, especially when it came to fucking. She seemed to know it all, what was pleasurable, where certain muscles were and what they did, and how many of her male friends wanted to be fucked all the time and how they prepared for it.

Aaron came away with one word in his head, lube. Thankfully she left an hour later, kissing him on both cheeks and declaring, "You're going to be the best stepson I've ever had."

He wanted to ask her how many she'd had already but he decided against it. She was a character. He liked her.

Aaron looked inside the kitchen window and saw Dave studying a cookbook. Several of them were open around him and he wore an expression of blissful intensity. Aaron backed off. He had the feeling Dave was enjoying his solitude. This gave him an idea. He had been dying to get his hands on the garden. Alberto had been doing a pretty good job, but it was huge for just one man and Aaron always did his best thinking with his hands in dirt.

He found a potting shed behind the pool cabana and began sorting through the tools he'd need. He kept thinking about the conversations he'd overheard at the warehouse. He tried not to worry but it was hard.

Man, being me was tough enough when I had the loan sharks on my back. They're like a piece of cake compared with actual mob guys!

The garden itself seemed to represent Aaron and his new life. It was neither English, nor was it quite tropical. He was no longer the Aaron he'd been . . . but he wasn't quite Troy either. He was somewhere in between. The future garden would represent this, he decided, since it seemed to already reflect two completely different, yet compatible styles at work. He started with the roses and this proved to be a necessary project. He pinched off the dead heads, cutting some of the roses back to their hips. He worked hard and fast, leaving some of the rose heads to live out their lives.

As he pruned, he could hear the drum of bees around him.

There must have been a hive some place close. He started to bag up his cuttings, when he heard a voice.

"What are you doing?"

He straightened. It was Dave. Seeing him again made Aaron smile.

"Pruning."

Dave gaped at him. "Since when do you know anything about gardening?" He shook his head. "You are one surprise after another lately." He jerked his thumb over his shoulder. "Dinner's ready."

"You cooked for me?" As the two men took the tools to the shed and dumped the trash in the bins lined up beside it, he felt Dave stiffen.

"I always cook for you."

Aaron looked him in the eye. "I will never take that for granted."

Dave's astonished look was bothersome. What in hell had this wonderful man ever seen in his selfish brother? His heart sank a little. *Troy must be one goddamned genius in the sack . . . shit, how in the hell can I measure up to that?*

They sat eating delicious angel hair pasta in the dining room, with a chilled bottle of white wine and garlic bread. Dave seemed quiet, until Aaron asked a few gentle questions about his work. Dave relaxed a little, talking about the new yoga studio and his geriatric students.

"You should build a studio here," Aaron said. Dave's mouth hung open.

"Do you really mean that?"

"Of course I mean it." They began to talk about it. Dave's passion ignited Aaron's enthusiasm. He wanted to help Dave make it happen.

"I thought we could use the pool cabana . . . maybe convert it as soon as the party is over," Dave said. "Speaking of which, I have calls to make." He pushed himself away from the table, but he seemed reluctant to end the meal.

"You're such a good cook," Aaron told him, thinking how he'd go check a few things out on the Internet later. Surely there was information on gay sex.

Dave smiled. "Thanks." He was in shorts tonight, nice and tight. They hugged his ass beautifully. He'd thrown a navy sleeveless T-shirt on top. It stretched across his taut chest, played up the muscles in his arms. Aaron thought about taking it off. Maybe if he took off his own T-shirt . . . Dave would take off his. It wouldn't hurt just to look at him a bit.

"It's hot," Aaron said. "Why don't we take off our shirts?" Aaron pulled his off and threw it aside. He hadn't had the chance to work out like Dave, but he knew he was in pretty good shape, despite being thinner.

Dave threw him an admiring glance. "You've lost weight," he said. "You stopped drinking those stupid muscle shakes?"

Uh-oh. Aaron grinned and changed the subject.

"Your turn?" Aaron suggested lightly. Come on, come on, take it off, baby. I just want to look at you.

Dave shrugged and pulled off the T-shirt in one tug. His muscles moved hypnotically under his smooth skin as he did, his nipples brown and stiff sat in his perfect pectorals.

Aaron swallowed. Dave was so hot. How could Troy have left him? How could he have wanted any other man?

Dave was eating again, taking the last piece of bread from the basket.

He seemed unaware of the effect he was having on Aaron. "Oh shit," he said suddenly, "the salad." He jumped up and walked into the kitchen, giving Aaron another glimpse of that perfectly round, hard ass of his. Maybe Dave would like to get fucked. Um . . . Aaron thought he could handle that, drilling his hard cock into that ass, running his hands all over that smooth well-muscled flesh as he did. Perhaps he'd yank back all that dark hair as he did, get him on his knees again to suck him like before.

What in hell is wrong with me? Where is all this raw emotion coming from? I've never wanted anyone like that . . . . let alone a man.

Dave returned with the salad. "Troy? Are you all right?"

Aaron glanced up at Dave. "Sure. Why?"

"You look, I don't know, strange." Dave helped himself to the salad.

"Do you remember the first time?" It came out quite naturally.

"The first time with you?"

"Your first time?" Aaron waited. Maybe he'd learn something about what he was like in bed, what he wanted in bed.

"Sure. Why are you asking?"

"Did you get fucked?"

He grinned. "Yeah. You know I got fucked."

"Did you like it, the first time?" He held his breath.

"Not at first. It was rather uncomfortable. The guy was gorgeous though . . ." He laughed. "So, I got over it."

"Then you like it?"

"Like what, getting fucked?"

"Yeah, getting fucked."

"Sure, but you never want to fuck me."

"I don't?"

"Troy, you *never* want to fuck me. You always want me to top. You love being fucked, and that's okay. I told you it doesn't matter. I like it both ways."

"What if I was . . . to . . ." he put down his fork. "I think I want to fuck you."

Dave's eyes widened. "Now?"

"Yeah." Aaron stood. "Right now."

"Troy, I thought you said that we were going to go no sex for a while?"

"We will. I promise. Just not tonight, okay?"

Dave pushed his plate back.

"Don't move."

Dave smiled uncertainly.

Aaron came around to the back of his chair. He placed his hands on Dave's shoulders, massaging them slowly.

"Um, that's nice."

"We got any oil?"

"Sure, upstairs. Where it always is. Are you sure you're all right? You're acting so weird tonight."

"I'll give you a massage." Aaron couldn't believe he was saying this. He just wanted to touch him, to run his hands all over him. He wanted to see his skin gleam. It was suddenly an obsession.

Dave started to get up.

"No, I'll ah . . . be right down. Where is the oil?"

"In the medicine cabinet."

Aaron ignored Dave's strange expression, ran upstairs and got the oil. His cock was so hard. He rubbed it a little though the material. "Sorry, brother, tonight he's mine. All the way. I can do this. I can fuck him, no problem." He smiled to himself on the way back downstairs. *No problem at all.*

Dave was still sitting there at the table. Aaron came around behind him once again. He splayed some mildly scented oil on his hands and began to massage Dave's shoulders again. He closed his eyes and moved his oily fingers over his chest. When he touched his nipples and circled them with the oil, they stiffened delightfully. He found touching them like that excited him, excited them both.

Aaron pulled and tugged Dave's nipples just a little and Dave's head went back. He moaned softly. Aaron swallowed. He wanted to look but closing his eyes helped him to sink into the mood. "Undo your zipper," Aaron coaxed. "I want you to stroke your cock, make it hard for me. God, you're so beautiful. Do it."

Aaron heard the zipper go down on the shorts.

"Is it in your hands?"

"Yeah," Dave breathed.

"Stroke it, baby. Make it hard for me."

"Halfway there, Troy."

Aaron continued to run his hands over Dave's arms and chest, pausing over those nipples that were so erect. He took a breath and pulled Dave's chair around. Dave's skin glistened with oil, and his cock stood straight out in his hand. It was the most erotic thing Aaron had ever seen.

Dave looked up at him. "Baby, please," he whispered.

Aaron straddled his legs and sat on his thighs. Dave's hard on pressed against his stomach. Aaron placed his hands on each side of Dave's face. He looked into those eyes and lowered his mouth to his. They kissed gently for a moment then Dave's passion peaked, and he roughly yanked Aaron forward, one hand in his hair and the other on his ass. Their kissing grew wild and out of control. Dave stood, lifted him up into his arms. Aaron's legs were wrapped around his waist and they hit the wall. Dave struggled to undo Aaron's pants.

It was out of control. Aaron couldn't think anymore. He let his legs down and hastily stripped off his jeans. Dave tore down Aaron's underwear and clutched his ass cheeks. "Lube!" Dave cried out.

Aaron had brought some down with the oil. "On the table." He was breathing hard as they stumbled together to the table and Dave got the lube.

Aaron took it. "Me. I want to do it . . . I want to lube you and I want to fuck that pretty ass." Aaron pressed Dave to his knees. He took a handful of his dark hair in his fist and yanked his mouth close to his cock. "Suck it. Suck me like you did before."

Dave took Aaron's cock into his mouth.

Aaron gasped. He reached out and held onto the table, his knees like rubber. His cock was enraptured, pulsing and alive as Dave's lips moved up and down his shaft. "Stop, stop . . ." Aaron pulled away, went to his knees, too. "If you keep doing that, I'm going to come. Turn around. Get on all fours." He spread lube in his hand, delighting in touching Dave's tight round ass. He flirted with Dave's hole for a moment. He wasn't sure what to do, how far to go. He pushed one lubed finger up into him and then went deeper.

Dave grunted.

Was that pleasure?

Another finger. He moved it in and out a little and waited for some sign that he was doing it right. Dave moaned.

"Is that good?"

"Fucking good. Go on, fuck me with your fingers. Hook them . . . yeah, like that. God, it's been so long . . . go on . . . shit, condom?" Dave glanced at him over his shoulder, his chest heaving.

"Why?"

"Why? You know why."

"No, I don't. I . . ."

"Fuck, Troy. You're not fucking me without a condom." He pushed him away and lay down flat on his stomach. "Not with your history."

"Fuck you, Dave!"

Dave didn't comment.

Aaron's anger and frustration turned to sadness. "I'm sorry," he whispered. He lay beside him on the floor and stroked his hair. "I'm so sorry for what he put you through. If you'd been mine, I would have spent my time worshipping you. You are so beautiful."

Dave looked up at him. "What are you talking about, Troy?" He got off the floor. "Now you're talking like you're a different man, referring to yourself as he? Christ, can't you take responsibility for your own actions?"

"I mean . . . I mean, the man I was. I've changed, Dave. I am a different man. Can't you feel it?"

Dave met his gaze. "You've done this before, Troy, acted

like you've reformed. It never lasts long."

"Damn," Aaron wasn't really listening anymore. He could only think of Dave. He wanted him. "Don't we have any condoms in the house? We could . . ."

"I've had it for tonight."

"You don't want me anymore?" Aaron looked at him, his feelings hurt.

"Christ, Troy," he pleaded, "Don't do this to me. Stop torturing me. I feel as if I'm drowning."

Aaron felt his pain. *Damn you, Troy, how could you? You've put this guy through hell.* Aaron could see it in his face. "I'm sorry." That's all he could say.

"I can't do this again with you. You suck me in, make me believe you really love me, and then you . . . well . . . you become *you* again. I was yours, Troy, but now, I'm not sure anymore. Prove to me you can be celibate, then we'll talk about finding a condom."

Aaron watched Dave pick up his clothes and leave the room. "Damn," he whispered. He'd never felt like this before. He'd never wanted anyone this way before. The need inside him was more than he'd expected. A need for his brother's husband. He closed his eyes. Was he falling in love? He didn't know, but he knew he was completely enraptured with lust, a craving Dave no longer seemed prepared to satisfy.

CHAPTER TEN

D ave lay in the empty bed. He tried to relax enough to fall asleep. He had chastised himself enough already. It was time to take a break from the 'Dave, you are one big idiot party.'

"When the hell are you going to smarten up, little brother, and leave that jerk?" Jeremy had asked him the last time he'd ended up on his doorstep.

Jeremy had had a hard time with him being gay when Dave had come out in his teens. Dave met Troy shortly after Jeremy came around and accepted that it wasn't 'just a phase,' as he'd hoped. His older brother had never liked Troy from day one. He thought him rude, and unpredictable. Sure, Troy could be arrogant, unfeeling at times, but Dave understood him. Growing up with Darren could have easily been a case study in the encyclopedia of dysfunctional relationships.

Troy told him things that he never told anyone about what it was like being the son of Darren Mayer. It was not pretty. Troy had developed all kinds of defense mechanisms which turned out to be very unattractive when he was in one of his 'moods.' Underneath, Troy was a hurt little boy who couldn't bear to mention his mother, a mother he'd been torn from at a young age. Often, Troy told David, "I feel like there's a part of me missing." David never really understood that.

When he was growing up, Darren was rarely there for Troy. Troy was reared by his stoic grandfather and frigid housekeeper. Neither one of them had much affection for the boy. Their firm belief in the 'spare the rod, spoil the child' philosophy resulted in Troy receiving regular beatings for very minor infractions. Dave knew that a lot of Troy's unattractive characteristics came from his childhood. Troy could be self-centered and egotistical. He could do things just for the pleasure of inflicting pain on others, and he had a constant need for reassurance and affection.

When it came to his father, Troy was like a puppet on a string. Either he was terrified of him or had a constant need for his approval. Just a telephone call from Darren could set Troy off, cause him to have an anxiety attack and throw up until all he could do was heave.

When the barriers were stripped away though, Troy could be sweet, and loving. He had a quirky sense of humor and was a pleasure to be with, funny, and intelligent, even child-like. The intensity of the love Troy showed him was revealed in those tender and rare moments. Those moments were real, and it was that he couldn't let go of.

Yes, he was a fool, just like Jeremy told him. He was a fool in love, but he'd seen a change in Troy lately. Troy seemed different. It was like he was really trying. It was like he was someone else completely. He was kinder to everyone. He was less stressed, but he was also more distant. It was like touching a stranger, at once exciting and new, and at the same time, it felt like Troy was pulling away from him.

This was probably just temporary. With Troy, Dave was always waiting for the other shoe to drop. He was promising so many things, but it would be impossible really for Troy to keep those promises.

As he lay there, wide awake, Dave made a decision. As much as it hurt, as much as he wanted to feel the man he loved inside him tonight, he could no longer be Troy's fool. This would be Troy's last chance. If Troy could go a month without cheating, go a month without sex all together, if he could make that sacrifice, then maybe . . . just maybe he really meant it this time.

If Troy broke this pact, Dave was finished.

It was this resolution that kept his eyes open in the

darkness, this absolute certainly that this time he meant it. If he had any self-respect at all, he had to follow through. Love was no longer enough.

With a sigh, Dave sat up in bed. He ran a hand through his hair. He looked at the moon shining through the window of the guest bedroom and he contemplated life without Troy. It looked empty just like the bed he lay in, but at least it held a certain dignity, a dignity born of truth.

He swallowed. He wouldn't shed any more tears over Troy for now. He'd save them for the day he packed his bags and walked out the door. And if Troy was true to form, that was just a few weeks away.

Dave seemed stressed out about the party preparations. For almost a week, they moved about the house like polite room-mates. Dave fielded calls from caterers and from Darren's secretary who seemed to have an ever-changing list of requirements.

Aaron worked his job but found that Darren shut him out of the important meetings. At home, Dave shut him out. Period.

His only respite was working in the garden. He found it to be the perfect refuge and loved how much Alberto responded to his suggestions. They cut back the bamboo that threatened to strangle some of the more delicate roses and Aaron was pleased when Alberto suggested a compost.

"I think it's a great idea."

Alberto looked shocked. Clearly the man was unused to Troy validating his opinions. They discussed replacing a few struggling plants with California natives, especially in the hard-to-water areas bordering on their neighbor's property behind them.

Aaron was stunned to learn that the bees belonged to the

Sooky Goldman Nature Preserve. He had to stop himself from remarking that he had no idea the Mayer family property bordered wild parkland. As soon as he got to a computer, he Googled Sooky Goldman and was impressed that the six hundred acre preserve serviced over 10,000 school children a year, educating them about plants and animals. He wondered if they needed volunteer landscapers and called them. He got a voice mail message and left his contact number.

Meanwhile, Dave kept party-planning. Aaron encouraged him. He wouldn't have had a clue about how to go about it all had it been left to him.

"And you're really okay about Ambrosia handling it?" Dave asked for the fourth time. Aaron had no idea who in the hell Ambrosia was but simply said he had no problem with it at all.

The following Saturday night, the house was filled with people.

Dave had snapped at him a little for being in the garden so long. "You need to get ready."

Aaron never took long to shower and dress. He felt a bit tense, in spite of the long day planting and pruning. He shrugged out his tired muscles under the shower. He thought about jerking off . . . no. He wouldn't.

As he dried off and dressed, he caught a glimpse of Dave rushing downstairs. He looked so handsome. Aaron followed him into the already crowded living room. He didn't know any of them, but they all seemed to know who he was. Matt had been invited, as had management people from the warehouse.

Aaron was not exactly thrilled to see Joe Carson show up, though. The first chance he got, he pulled Dave aside and asked him why he'd invited him.

"I didn't," Dave said. "Your father did."

"Great, he's drunk. I hope he doesn't make an ass out of himself."

Dave leaned down with his lips close to Aaron's ear. "That's why you don't fuck the employees."

Aaron sighed as Dave walked off. He looked wonderful as usual, dressed in black pants and a teal colored shirt, open at the neck. He drew a lot of admiring glances. Aaron wondered if Troy had been insecure having a husband that good-looking.

Matt had seen the exchange. "Everything all right?" he asked.

"Sure."

"Must be uncomfortable with Carson here. I can't believe you told Dave."

"I wanted to be honest. Anyway, he already knew."

Matt sipped his drink. He didn't seem surprised. "I haven't heard any more about our deal yet, have you?"

"Well," Aaron said absently, not sure what to say, "ah, I'm sure you'll hear when I do."

Nancy came to stand beside him now, just a little tipsy. He introduced her to Matt. She was wearing a lowcut black dress a little shorter than was fashionable and a pair of ridiculously high heeled red pumps. He had no idea how she walked in those things, or how soon they'd be doing the backstroke in the pool.

"Don't they hurt?" he asked, looking at her shiny heels.

Matt got distracted by a couple he knew and moved off.

"They kill," she said, laughing.

"Why do you wear them then?"

"Darren likes them, and they make me look hot."

Aaron shook his head.

"Want to try a pair? They look great when you're naked."

He laughed. "You kidding? I couldn't even stand up in those things. And I doubt they're Dave's thing."

She linked her arm in his. "Speaking of the Greek god, Dave looks good enough to eat."

Shit, was Dave Greek? No, he was half Italian . . . or was it Spanish? It might be a good thing to check on. He knew he'd been born in LA but as for his heritage? He'd only heard him speak English.

"Yeah, he does look good enough to eat," Aaron said.

"Everyone here would love to take him to bed."

"Um, so it seems."

"What's with you and that guy?" She was looking over at Joe Carson.

"Why? What?" Aaron met her gaze. "Nothing."

"He's been staring at you all night. You do the nasty with him or something?"

Shit, she was perceptive. "No," Aaron said. "It's nothing."

"Okay. Just one thing, honey, he couldn't hold a candle to Dave. Look at them."

"I know that."

"If you're bored, just spice up the sex a little. Don't play away from home. You have too much to lose. Don' t be afraid to use toys. I have some great ones."

Aaron nodded. "I'll remember that."

"Come dance with your old stepmonster," she coaxed.

"If you take off those things," he replied, looking at the shoes.

"Done." She leaned down and slipped off her shoes.

Dave paused when he noticed that Troy was among the dancers on the dance floor. He was doing the twist with Nancy, and actually looking like he was having a good time, which was surprising. Troy didn't even like to dance. He'd had a hell of time even getting him to dance with him at their wedding. He had to be drunk.

The pop country band he'd hired was going over big. He'd decided to do things casual, finger foods, barbeque, open bar and dancing. It was Darren's style.

It was a nice night and people were mingling inside and outside. Some had brought their bathing suits and were in the pool or the hot tub.

Darren had been his typical asshole self and basically ignored Nancy all evening, talking business with his associates in the games room.

Joe Carson had been glaring at him all night. He'd noticed Troy had kept away from the guy and hadn't disappeared once all evening. Dave had all he could do not to walk over to Joe and tell him to fuck off. He held back since Darren had invited the guy, deciding not to make a scene as long as Carson kept his mouth shut.

But Troy, dancing . . . that was very strange.

People began to leave around three in the morning, and it was actually dawn before the place cleared out. Aaron did a last-minute check around to make sure there was no one who had passed out somewhere. Actually, the only one he found asleep was Dave. He lay on the sofa, an arm flung over his face. So cute. Aaron took a blanket and placed it over him, then leaned down and kissed his hair. It was silky and smelled of some mild fragrance.

He swallowed and backed away. He felt almost protective of him, with this feeling that no matter what happened, he'd let no one hurt him. "Sleep well, angel," he whispered, and went up to bed.

Aaron crawled into bed with his laptop and went to check out pictures of buff gay men on some site where they confessed their erotic fantasies or told stories about their sexual experiences.

Every story he read, he thought about acting out with Dave, and every guy he checked out, he compared to Dave. None of them passed. He finally shut down the computer, his cock as hard as rock.

He turned off the light as daylight streamed in through the window and squeezed his swollen cock a little. He eventually fell asleep, still hard, with an image of Dave sitting at the dining room table, his torso slick with oil. In his dream, Aaron ran the tip of his tongue around each of Dave's erect nipples slowly. He licked them, teasing them, enjoying the feeling of their stiffness on his tongue. "Dave," he moaned.

Strong arms wrapped around him and he felt a hard cock stab up into him, over and over. He cried out then moaned with need. "Yes, fuck me. Fuck me." Over and over the cock moved in and out of him, from side to side, coaxing sounds from deep inside.

You want me, don't you?

Yes, yes . . . oh fuck . . . yes.

Aarons' eyes snapped open. He was alone, breathing hard. He glanced at the alarm. It was two in the afternoon. Shit. He swung his legs over the side of the bed and left the room. He headed down the hallway then paused to see Dave, naked except for a towel around his waist. He stood in the bathroom, brushing his teeth.

Aaron walked into the bathroom, trying not to ogle him. "Hey."

Dave wiped his mouth on a towel and smiled at him.

"Congratulations on the party last night. It went over well. You just get up?"

"No, I went for a jog then hopped in the shower."

He smelled amazing. "What is that?" Aaron breathed in the scent.

"Shampoo." He laughed.

"It smells like cologne."

"Nope. Just me." He grinned and went to leave.

Aaron blocked his way. "Don't leave."

"Troy. We said a month, remember?"

"Yeah, and it's been a week, and I'm in hell. How about you, baby?"

He brushed past him. "I'll be fine."

Aaron closed his eyes and sighed. "Great!"

They spent a lazy Sunday, swimming in the pool and just talking. Dave was going to start work on the pool cabana for his new studio first thing in the morning. Aaron was so pleased for him. He'd deduced that Troy had been against it. Why?

He'd encourage Dave's dreams. He wanted to know more about him, but he was afraid to ask questions about things he was supposed to know. He'd already goofed on asking Dave about his first sexual encounter.

"Tell me some stories about you as a boy," Aaron said as they sat side by side on the lawn chairs.

"Come on." Dave grinned, adjusting his sunglasses on his nose. "You know them all."

"Tell me your favorite memory as a boy."

He shook his head with a grin. "You know what it was. It was when my uncle took me in the fire truck."

"Your uncle was a fireman."

"Yeah, you met my uncle. Remember, at the party for my father's retirement."

"Yeah, right, and your dad, does he miss his job?"

"Are you kidding? He's still working all the time. You know he can't stop."

Aaron wanted to slap himself. "What made you want to become a personal trainer?"

Dave stared at him a moment. "After Dad had his heart at-tack, I got really interested in staying in shape. You know how

I was in high school then I got the scholarship. My dad still hasn't forgiven me for not trying out for pro soccer."

"You played soccer. But you're happy right, doing what you do?"

Dave reached over and took his hand. "You know you've never asked me that question before."

"I want to know." Aaron caressed his fingers.

"Yeah, I'm happy. I make a great living, get to travel, meet interesting people."

"I want you to be happy, David." Aaron met his eyes. "I want to make you happy."

Dave smiled. "I want to make you happy, too."

"You do," Aaron nodded. "I've always felt so alone. Now that I've met you, I don't feel that way anymore." *Shit, this was true. This was him, not Troy.* The way his mother had been as he'd been growing up. She'd never taken care of him. He'd been the parent and she was too sick to really love him. He'd always been alone.

"Hey," Dave said, reaching over to catch as tear as it ran down Aaron's face. "You're crying."

Aaron wiped at his tears. "I love you." He met his eyes. "Jesus, I never thought it possible. Dave, I love you."

David smiled. "I know that, babe. I know that in spite of everything, deep down you love me. Let's start again. Let's make a clean slate and . . ."

Aaron sniffed and sat back in his seat. "We will, after I prove to you that I can be faithful. Only two and a half weeks to go."

Dave groaned and they both laughed.

After that Sunday afternoon, things seemed different. Dave went to work, came home, worked on the studio space and spent quiet evenings with Troy. They talked more. Sometimes they watched a movie, other times, they played cards. They spent time in the garden together. Dave loved how Troy seemed excited about his new plants.

He also had suggestions for a macrobiotic garden to plant around the studio. That was a wonderful surprise. So was the fact that his husband wanted to volunteer at the nature preserve behind their property and how Troy confessed to being hurt that nobody had returned his calls yet.

Troy was very supportive about the Pilates studio, which was now completely renovated. Stacey Adler, the woman Dave had met in London, was the first client he trained in it. Troy had surprised him by bringing a small bonsai into the studio as a good luck gift. It had tiny jade elephants drinking from a stream and an old man fishing with a pole from a bridge.

It was simply stunning.

"Where did you buy it?" Dave asked, entranced.

"I didn't buy it. I made it." Troy gave one to Stacey when she begged him for it. Then Nikko Watanabe, a close friend of Stacey's, wanted one. Troy trotted around next door and left one on their neighbor's doorstep. Gone were the days when Troy waged inexplicable wars with the neighbors.

Dave was pleased he could bring clients to train at the house whenever he wanted. He no longer worried about Troy screaming at people about their mere presence on his property, or their noise level.

These days, Troy's laughter came easily. It was so peaceful. At night, they talked about their dreams. As the evenings waned, they would go their separate ways and sleep alone. One night, Troy retired with a book entitled *The Undaunted Garden: Planting for Weather-Resilient Beauty.*

Dave teased him about it. "I've never seen you crack open a book."

"Yes, you have."

"No, I haven't." Dave started to laugh. "Can a garden actually be undaunted?"

"I don't think it's so funny. I think the title is apt," Troy said, a little stiffly.

"How so?"

"I'm undaunted," Troy responded. "About *us*."

Dave didn't know what to say. He wanted to cave in and invite the man back into his bed, but he didn't.

Dave felt more optimistic about his future with Troy than he ever had. He had no idea what had happened. It was like Troy had transformed himself into someone else altogether, and Dave couldn't get enough of him.

With only three nights of their sexual sabbatical to go, Dave knew that they were going to make it. When Nancy called the house saying she was lonesome one evening because Darren had left town on business, Dave hesitated before checking with Troy about inviting her over for dinner.

Troy could be so weird about company. He surprised him by insisting they invite her. He was charming over their meal of *coq au vin*, which Troy found out was Nancy's favorite.

Dave felt as if he could start to breathe. The man he'd married seemed to be full of surprises these days. As a slightly tipsy Nancy regaled them with tales of her flight attendant classes from her recently single existence, he and Troy laughed, frequently exchanging hot glances.

God, I want him . . .

Dave was already anticipating the night when he could hold Troy again and make love to him. It had been torture these last few weeks but somehow, it had been the best thing they'd ever done.

When he got the call as his office that day, he couldn't believe it. It was Samuel Devereux's personal assistant. Devereux was a celebrated movie star, and right now, he was as hot as hot could be. Devereux had put him on retainer last year, paying him to be on call any time he needed him.

"David, Miranda Redding here. How are we?"

She always talked like that.

"I'm well, thanks."

"Samuel needs body fantastic. Has to be in London for three days, leaving tomorrow afternoon. He won't go without you. You know how he gets."

"Tomorrow?" Dave practically moaned.

"Problem?"

"No, no, I'll ah . . . be there."

"He'll send the car round your place at nine tonight as usual. See you then, David, *chéri*."

"Right." David hung up. *Great timing.*

There were a lot of boxes being unloaded today and for some reason, his father hadn't come into work. People were asking Aaron a million questions, and although he'd picked up a lot since he'd been at the warehouse, he still didn't know how to answer them all. Of course that meant the he had to ask Joe, who took every opportunity to get into a deep discussion about his and Troy's former sex life.

When the phone rang on his desk later in the afternoon, he'd had it. He picked it up and barked, "Don't ask me any questions. I don't know, okay?"

"You don't know if you love me?"

It was Dave. Aaron smiled and softened his voice. "Hey, baby. Yes, I know that. I love you. I'm sorry. What are you doing?"

"Oh, the usual routine. Rough day?"

"Stock has been coming in all day, a lot of stock, and people are running around going nuts."

"Darren not in to help?"

"Nope, haven't seen him. What's up, beautiful?"

"I have a question. How about we cut our sex fast short by

one day?"

Aaron's heart sped up. "What? Why?"

"I've got to leave tomorrow, three days in London."

"Oh, no."

"Sorry. Anyway, either we cheat and cut it short a day or . . . wait until I get back. What do you think?"

Aaron gripped the phone. He'd read all he could read. He'd suffered all he could suffer. No matter how they made love, Dave could never hurt him. He wanted to explore everything with him, and he couldn't wait three more days. "Do you trust me now? Have I proven myself to you, baby?"

"Yes."

"What time can you get home?" Aaron could hardly breathe.

"I can get out of here by four."

"Make it three-thirty."

"I'll see you there."

"I love you."

"Love you back."

Aaron sat rigid in his seat, eyes closed. He smiled, phone still in his hand. *He trusts you now . . . happy? All you've done is lie to him. You're not Troy. You're not the man he married. You are a fraud.*

"How sweet."

Aaron sat upright. His eyes flew open at the sound of a voice. "Joe. What are you doing in here?"

Joe came in and closed the door. "What a fake you are. You really sound sincere when you talk like that. I assume that was David, or do you have another fish on the hook now?"

"Joe." Aaron stood up. "I don't want to hear this. Just . . . stop it."

"You sounded like that when we made love in the hotel. You sound like that when my cock was in—"

"Enough!" Aaron said. "I don't love you. I don't want you. If I said that, I was out of my mind. Now, stop this, Joe."

111

Joe sank down in the chair and put his face in his hands. "I can't stand it. I'll kill myself."

Oh, Lord.

Joe sobbed in Aaron's office for a half hour before he could quiet him. He didn't know how to handle the guy's breakdown. Then something came up in shipping he was called to figure out. It was almost five before he got out of there, and then he had to practically sneak out the back door.

As he drove toward home, his mind was on Dave. It had been on Dave all afternoon. He stopped at the pharmacy, bought lube and condoms and some massage oil. Tonight was the night. Tonight was the night that he tossed away all his inhibitions and gave himself to David completely. He was ready. He tried not to focus on the betrayal. He was better for him than Troy. He could love him better. He knew that but Dave would not be making love to him tonight. He'd be making love to Troy. For better or worse, he'd call out his brother's name in the heat of the moment, not his, never his, never Aaron.

Chapter Eleven

When Dave heard Troy drive up, he walked to the window and pulled the curtain back. He breathed a sigh of relief. He'd been worried. He expected Troy to be home already. It was almost six o'clock.

Dave waited, wondering why Troy wasn't getting out of the car. He just sat there, the motor idling. Dave walked outside and came around to the driver side. The window was open. He looked in at Troy.

"Are you all right? What are you doing sitting there?"

Troy looked at him. He looked miserable. Suddenly he reached out and clutched onto David's arm. "You love me, don't you?"

"Of course," he said. Troy's hold on his arm had started to hurt. "Troy?"

"No matter what, no matter what, God, could you forgive me anything?" Tears streamed down his face and the hold got tighter.

"Ouch, damn it, Troy." He pulled back. "What's got into you?" He rubbed his arm then softened his voice. "Sweetheart, what is it? What happened?"

"I'm scared to lose you."

"You won't lose me."

Troy lowered his head. "Yes, yes, I will." His chest heaved and he started to sob.

Dave opened the car door and pulled him out. He held him for a few minutes until the tears started to subside. "Baby, what's wrong?" He held him away and looked down into his face.

Troy shook his head, wiped at his face. "Nothing. Nothing is wrong. Just a hard day, that's all."

Dave threw his arm around him. "Let's go inside. I thought you might be hungry. I let Manuela go home. I made that shrimp salad you like."

Aaron felt like a fool. He washed his face and glanced at his reflection in the mirror. What had caused him to react like that? When he'd pulled up in front of the house, it hit him. What if Dave found out he wasn't Troy? He'd never forgive him. He knew it. He'd throw him out in the cold. He'd hate him. It would be just too cruel.

As he came downstairs, he stopped to admire the table Dave had set for him. No one had ever done anything for him, let alone take time to set a beautiful table.

They sat together across from one another with the candles lit. They ate in silence, but the silence was comfortable, reassuring. Aaron ate little. He waited until Dave finished the last bite then he said, "Let's go upstairs."

Dave looked over at him. "You didn't eat much."

Aaron stood up. "I can't think of anything but making love to you," he said softly. "I'll eat later." He didn't wait for a response. He just turned and headed for the stairs, discarding his clothing as he went. When he heard Dave scrape his chair back and follow; his heart hammered against his ribcage.

He turned at the top of the steps and Dave was right in front of him. "I went to the pharmacy," he began, "and —"

David never gave him time to finish. He lowered his head and pressed his mouth against his. "Shush," he said, pulling Aaron into his arms, his hands moving over his naked flesh. "Don't talk," he murmured against his hair. "Show me. Show me how much you love me."

Aaron took Dave's hand and led him into the bedroom. Any trepidation he might have had slipped away when he looked into those eyes. Slowly, he opened his shirt. He didn't want the moment to run too fast. He wanted to hold onto it forever.

Dave seemed to sense that. He didn't hurry him. He waited patiently until Aaron got to the last button. Aaron slowly peeled off the shirt and threw it aside. There was a little sound that came from Dave's throat, somewhere in between a sigh and a moan.

"Wait," Aaron said. He dashed over to the bed and switched on the lamp. He dumped all the stuff from the pharmacy onto the bed, then came back. "I want to see you. I want to look at you. Is that all right?"

Dave nodded, something in his throat working.

Aaron ran his fingers over his chest, pausing at one of his nipples. He passed his thumb over it twice and smiled, moving his fingers down to David's jeans. He undid the snap and rode the zipper down. He could hardly believe that this man was his.

Dave took off his shoes but then stood quietly again.

Aaron pulled the jeans down and Dave stepped out of them, pushing them aside with his foot. He stood there in white briefs, his cock barely contained by the material and Aaron slowly ran his fingers over the outline of the bulge. There was a stain forming, a definite sign that Dave was as much in need as Aaron was.

"Touch me," Dave pleaded, his voice shaking.

Aaron ran his fingers down Dave's chest to his abs. He slid them inside the waistband and pushed down the briefs. Dave's cock sprang forward, and Aaron took it in his hand. He wanted to touch it. He wanted to taste it . . . to feel its texture . . . to feel it inside of him.

He raised his gaze. Dave's eyes were closed. Aaron squeezed his cock in his fist and Dave moaned, swerving a little. Aaron kissed his throat, his chest, licked his nipples just like in his dream then dropped to his knees.

He forgot everything he read on how to give a good blow-job. He shielded his teeth and swiped his tongue around the head of Dave's cock then leaned his head back at an angle and took it deeper into his mouth.

Dave's hand pressed onto his head. He grunted then again swayed as little. His hips moved, the hold on Aaron's head tightened and he groaned, "Yes, yes, fuck . . . suck it . . . oh God . . . yes. I've missed you so much."

Aaron held onto the base of his cock. The taste and the texture filled his mouth and he was consumed by it. His lips tightened, his tongue moved around, and he came up and off and then back down again. The sucking grew intense, Dave's hold on his head was intense, and there was nothing else in the world except Dave's beautiful cock in his mouth.

Strong hands now held his face still and Dave's erection moved frantically in and out of his mouth with a frenzied intensity. Then suddenly, he pulled back and out.

Aaron wiped the back of his mouth. Dave was beside him on the floor. He grabbed his waist, turned him around, onto his hands and knees. Aaron heard the top of the lube pop open. He knew what was about to happen.

"Relax," Dave said, one strong hand pressed on his neck as the other pushed his knees apart. "I can hold on. I want to make it good for you."

Aaron closed his eyes as Dave moved one finger against his anus. No one had ever touched him there. He tried not to flinch. A warm tongue touched it now, moving around, bathing it in, making him twitch a bit. "Oh God," he whispered. "What are you doing to me?"

"It will be cold at first. It will be warm after." A lubed finger flicked across his ass again and then wiggled up inside of him.

He grunted.

Deeper, the finger went deeper, invading him in a

forbidden place, a place more intimate than anywhere.

Another finger moving around, lubricating, and soothing, pushing against resistance. A buzzing sound.

"What's that?" He glanced over his shoulder.

"Something to open you up a bit, prepare you. It's been a while. You're so tight. God, you're going to feel good."

Hands moved over his body, reached under and fondled his cock then he felt something press against his opening and move up inside, something slick and slim, pulsing inside him. Aaron moaned. "Um, God . . . what is that?"

"Just a slim vibrator, something to make it easier for my cock." He pulled it forward a little then pressed it up inside again, turning it around a few times.

Aaron's entire body tingled. He wanted to close his legs. He closed his eyes, let out a cry. "Baby!"

Dave was still touching him everywhere, slowly jerking his cock, massaging his balls and moving that object up inside him. It was stretching him. It felt so good. Then the object moved out again and back in, faster now, in and out. Aaron cried out, his cock pulsing.

Dave held onto his cock. "Can't come yet, baby, not until I'm inside you." One hand on Aaron's back, the vibrator moved in and out of his ass in a slow, gentle fuck that had Aaron tearing at the carpet. "Tell me you want me," Dave whispered, kissing down his back, "tell me you want my cock."

"I want it . . . God, Dave, fuck me. Make me feel it."

The object slowly moved out of him, coaxing a low, long moan out of Aaron's chest. Dave didn't hesitate. His cock pressed at his entrance as he pulled him up a little more and plunged deep inside of him.

Aaron couldn't get his breath. Dave's cock was inside of him and the shooting sensations in his body caused him to shake all over. He cried out as their bodies slammed together.

Dave fucked him hard on his knees then turned him around as Aaron's cock pulsed and shot, and before he was finished, Dave was inside of him again, only this time with Aarons' legs over his shoulders.

Aaron moved with him now, as Dave pulled his legs up more and looked deep in his eyes. He slowed his pace, moving from side to side, hitting every damn sensitive spot he could. "Deeper," Aaron pleaded, his hips pumping. "Shit, deeper, harder." He moaned, his cock still pumping and then he looked up and saw Dave's face. His eyes closed, his teeth biting into his lower lip, head back. He let out a deep groan, his hips still swaying then he lowered Aaron's legs and fell on his side.

It was quiet and Aaron could hear the heavy beating of Dave's heart. He reached for his hand and Dave curled his fingers around his. This was sacred. Aaron didn't realize his cheeks were wet. He wiped his face hastily, didn't want Dave to see that he'd been crying during sex, crying from the intense emotions he felt.

He moved closer and placed his head on Dave's shoulder. He kissed it, his hand in his. "I love you."

Dave turned to look at him. "You don't have to say it. I know it."

"You've always known it, haven't you?"

He nodded. "I'm sorry for how you grew up. I was hoping that I'd love you so well, it would make up for it."

Aaron sucked in some breath. "You do. I want to be everything for you. I'm a changed man, Dave. I promise. I'll never hurt you again."

Dave wrapped him in his arms. "Then I'm a happy man."

"I wish you didn't have to go to London."

"Me, too, but I'm afraid it can't be helped."

"I'm starved," Aaron whispered.

Dave kissed the top of his head. "Me, too."

"You, too?" Aaron got up off the floor "You ate your supper."

"Whoever gets downstairs first gets to eat the rest of the salad," Dave rang out, jumping up as well.

Aaron raced him to the bedroom door and Dave kept pushing him back. They wrestled like that all the way down the stairs.

They ended up sitting on the kitchen floor naked in front of the refrigerator, sharing what was left of the salad. Dave positioned Troy between his open thighs. Troy leaned back against his chest while Dave fed him the salad from his fork.

When the plate was empty, Dave set it aside. He tightened his hold on Troy and tilted his head back to the side for a kiss. The kiss got a lot more passionate than he intended and Troy pushed him down on the floor on his back.

"I want to touch you, kiss every inch of you," he whispered.

Dave smiled, closing his eyes as Troy moved down over him, his tongue tasting him, swirling around his nipples and his cock. Finally, Troy took his hand and pulled Dave to his feet. "Let's go upstairs. Your ass is mine."

Dave grinned. "What if I say no?" he teased.

"I'll take it anyway." Troy slapped his ass once.

That brought laughter. "Think you can do it?"

"Get that fine ass of yours upstairs and I'll show you."

This was a side of Troy he'd never seen before. He liked it. He liked it a lot.

"Lay down on the bed," Troy told him upstairs. He stood there for a moment looking at him as Dave stretched. "Don't move."

"I'm not going anywhere."

Troy returned with two bathrobe ties. Dave laughed. "Oh,

kinky."

Troy tied his wrists to the headboard. "Keep your legs spread like that. Oh yeah, baby, did you ever think of posing for one of those magazines . . . you would have sold a million copies. You are so hot."

He laughed. "Glad you think so."

Troy spread some lube on his hand and crawled between his legs. "I want to take a picture of you. Can I?"

Dave let out a shout when the cold lube hit his ass. "Whoa . . . baby . . . if you want but not to show anyone."

Troy laughed, his finger quite aggressively probing him. As he inserted two fingers and began to move them in and out, he licked and then nibbled Dave's nipple. "I wouldn't. I want it for me."

Dave lifted his hips and moaned a little. "Um, anytime."

"You like that eh?" The fingers continued to do their work, and Troy reached for a condom. "You are turning me on so much. God, you look so hot tied like that. Dave, baby," he removed his fingers and leaned down to kiss him. Their tongues mingled and they both moaned a little, Dave's hips pushing upwards.

"Fuck me, babe."

Troy smiled, licking down his neck. "First a little time with these. Such a great chest, perfect nipples." He took one between his teeth and pulled, one hand roughly handling Dave's cock.

"Oh God," Dave cried out.

"Seems I found a sensitive spot," Troy laughed. He leaned back and took Dave's cock in his hand. He handled it, squeezed it, lifted it. "So big, so thick . . . so good inside me."

He reached over and pinched his nipple, pulled, roughly ran his fingers over both and Dave began to plead.

"Won't be long, baby." Troy lifted Dave's legs, lubed fingers up inside him again, hitting the prostrate. Dave thrashed.

Troy's cock entered him tentatively, as if he was having a religious experience.

"Troy, are you going to fuck me or not?"

Troy's mouth opened and he met Dave's gaze. He looked stunned, frozen for a moment. He whispered his name and then let go, fucking him like there was no tomorrow. They both came shortly after with a shout, Troy's hand on Dave's spent cock. Troy collapsed on Dave's stomach where he lay silent for the longest time.

"Troy? Are you all right? You haven't had a heart attack, have you?"

He lifted his head. "No," he said, "I'm okay. Stay like that. I want to take a picture." He got up and took the camera out of the drawer. He snapped a few pictures then jumped on the bed to show Dave. "You are so hot."

Dave kissed the top of his head. "As long as you think so."

Troy put the camera aside. He reached up and undid Dave's wrists then took his arms and wrapped them around him. "Hold me," Troy said. "Hold me like you'll never let me go."

Dave tightened his arms around him. "That was . . . bizarre at first. I thought you'd changed your mind about fucking me."

"I'm sorry. I . . . got caught up in the moment. You felt so good. It was so incredible. It was a little overwhelming fucking you."

Troy fell asleep a few minutes later and Dave lay there in the dark, holding him, trying to make sense of it all. From the moment they'd come upstairs, there'd been something different, something different about Troy. Even when he was inside of him . . . it was like . . . he wasn't the same person. Dave shook himself. He was losing his mind. Great sex would do that to a person.

CHAPTER TWELVE

Aaron didn't want to go to work. He wanted to go with Dave to the airport. "Three days," he moaned.

Dave kissed him. "I'll be back before you know it."

"I'll miss you so much." Aaron clung to him before he went out the door. "Will you phone me when you arrive in London?" he asked.

"We're on different time zones. I'll leave you a voice message, okay?"

"Okay. Be careful."

"You, too."

Aaron walked toward the car then ran back for another hug. Dave laughed, kissed him on the top of the head and waved him goodbye.

Aaron kept his gaze on Dave in the rearview mirror until he turned off onto the road. Everything had changed since he'd met Dave. And last night the world had turned on its axis. They belonged to each other now, and he couldn't wait for Dave to come back home so they could make love. All he wanted was Dave inside him, and to touch him. He'd lived out a fantasy last night, God, to have such a hot guy in restraints. Now that he'd done that, he was sure he could think of other fun stuff to do.

He printed the pictures he had taken and lay on the bed to admire them a few minutes. He lazily stroked his cock as he looked at them. He came hard and fast before taking a shower. He placed the photos under his pillow, thinking he could use those to keep him going until Dave came home.

He drove into the warehouse parking lot and glanced at the clock. Eight-thirty. He'd be counting the hours.

He saw his father briefly that day. Darren seemed to be in

a hurry and didn't have much to say. Luckily Joe had taken the day off, so it was a fairly easy workload. The evening brought loneliness, and loneliness caused him to worry about all kinds of things. He didn't even feel like working in the garden. He lay on the bed he'd shared with Dave, the man's scent still clinging to the sheets and stared at those photographs.

I don't wanna lose him, I don't wanna lose him . . .

Sleep eluded him. He kept waiting for Dave to call. Early the next morning he awoke to a voice message Dave had left in the middle of the night saying, "Arrived safe, beat. I love you." It made him smile.

He had lunch with Matt that day and tried to change the subject whenever Matt brought up this media deal thing. He wasn't quite sure what Troy had gotten into with this thing. He was hoping to find some documentation amongst his brother's things. So far, no such luck. It made him wonder. Was it real? Was it a scam? Wouldn't he have something on his hard drive concerning all this? He didn't want to start talking about something he had no idea about.

"Let's not talk business," he told Matt.

"Fine. How's Dave?"

"He's gone until tomorrow."

"Oh, where to this time?"

"London."

"You miss him." Matt grinned.

"Yes." He leaned forward. "I'm not the same guy I was, Matt. I realize I have all I need now. No more fucking around."

"Wow, you've grown a brain. I thought for sure you'd lose him."

"Thanks." Aaron laughed and gave him a punch in the arm. Then he sobered. "But you're right. He would have left me."

"I would have grabbed him."

"I would have killed you!" They both laughed.

An hour later, they were standing together in the parking lot. "Call me when you hear something," Matt said, before heading to his car. "Just waiting to transfer the money."

Aaron mumbled something then watched Matt drive off. He was pondering that when he got into his car. *Transfer what money?*

He stopped by Hashimoto Nursery on Sawtelle Avenue to pick up some new gardening supplies. Now that he and Alberto had created a credible compost heap, he wanted to buy more sod, fertilizer and a few more bonsai plants and tiny statues he enjoyed making for gifts. He was startled to see little butterflies and bears among the figurines. They reminded him sadly of his life in Los Osos. He took a deep breath. That seemed like such a long time ago.

Aaron turned and was shocked to run into Jake, his friend who'd given him a ride to the bus in Morro Bay, helping him to escape the loan sharks, so many weeks ago. The two men stared at one another.

Jake however, seemed uncertain if it was Aaron. He stared and squinted. Aaron peered into the man's eyes. His pupils were wildly dilated. Either he was on drugs, or he'd had a recent visit to an ophthalmologist. Knowing Jake as he did, he suspected the latter.

"Aaron?" he asked. "Is that you?"

Swallowing hard, Aaron said, altering his voice a little, "No, my name is Troy."

"I'm so sorry. Then you have a doppelgänger."

"No problem." Aaron smiled and kept moving. As he paid for his items, he noticed Jake across the counter space staring at him. Aaron bent his head to his wallet, counting out his cash. Of all the frickin' gin joints . . .

He hurried to his car, hands shaking as he loaded up his trunk. A stone butterfly fell out of one of the bags and tinkled to pieces on the ground. Aaron had a bad feeling something was about to change. He slammed the trunk shut and drove home, trying to convince himself to calm down.

Over a solitary meal of pasta and salad, he went through more of Troy's paperwork but could find nothing about the media deal with Matt. He was thrilled when Dave called, and they had a very brief conversation.

"I wish you were here, in my bed," Dave said. "Just one more sleep, baby. I'll call you if I can get an earlier flight."

Aaron went to bed, watching TV. He longed for Dave and felt haunted by strange night sounds. He heard a screech and a faint feline cry. An owl had caught a cat. He buried himself under the covers, trying not to panic. Dave's photographs lay on top of the bed next to him.

The next day, work went so well he felt almost relaxed. Darren had gone to Las Vegas on business and the tension level eased considerably for the entire staff. Aaron ordered pizza for everybody and over lunch, the mood seemed festive.

When he got home, Dave had left another message. He hated missing the man's calls and hated that Troy had insisted on Dave leaving messages with the service. He'd have to re-educate Dave and have him call the house phone or his cell phone only. He was happy to hear, however, that Dave would be home tomorrow probably early in the in the morning. That was great news. Aaron ate the frittata Manuela had prepared and combed through another of Troy's filing cabinets. There was nothing about any media deal.

He went to bed early. Once again, he had problems getting to sleep. He was anxious to see Dave, and excited that he was coming home tomorrow.

The telephone woke him. He squinted at the alarm clock and groaned. *Six thirty.* "Holy hell!" He reached over to pick it up and knocked it off the nightstand then worried it could be Dave. Had something happened to Dave? "Shit!" He reached down and picked up the receiver. "Yeah? Hello?"

"Troy, it's your father. We're going to need the money this week."

Aaron threw his legs over the side of the bed. "Money? What money?" He rubbed his eyes.

"Don't fuck around, Troy. You know what money, the two million, that's what money. Now, go and get it. Shipment is coming in end of the week."

Aaron was speechless.

"Are you there?"

"Ah, yeah . . . I'm here but . . ."

"Listen, you little fuck, you good-for-nothing, piece of shit, don't play games with me. You have it. Go and get it."

Aaron was taken aback. "Hey, wait, who in the hell do you think you're talking to? I have no idea what money you're talking about."

"Troy, if we don't have that money by the end of the week, they're going to kill us. They'll kill *you* and everyone around you. The shipment is in Saturday night. I'm going to need you to go down to the port and pick it up with one of the trucks, just like you did the last time. Santini swears we're square after you do this. Let's get it over with and be done with this fucker for good. He's strangling me."

Aaron narrowed his eyes. *Jesus Christ. Drugs?* He didn't want to be involved in this. "You go pick it up. I want nothing to do with it."

"Like shit! You will do as I tell you. They only want you. You know that. They trust you. Stop fucking around and get the money." The line went dead.

Aaron stared at the phone. Money? Did Troy hide money somewhere? His father had said two million. Troy had money in his bank account but nothing like two big ones. Shit, he had no idea where this money was. Mob money. It was fucking mob money.

He got out of bed, shaking. He'd had a bad feeling ever since running into Jake at the gardening store. What was the guy doing in LA? He thought for a moment. He had never told Jake that he had a twin and Jake always shopped at Hashimoto Nursery when he was in town. Jake had been the one to introduce Aaron to the place.

Aaron paced the bedroom. Had Jake recognized him? Would he ever tip off the loan sharks? No, he didn't think so. The guy had helped him get out of Dodge.

One problem at a time, he told himself. The biggest problem was the two million. Had Troy stolen mob money and run off somewhere, leaving him to hold the bag? Desperately, Aaron went online and checked the two accounts Troy had given him access to. He had almost a quarter of a million dollars between his mortgage and checking accounts and his credit card limit.

Not enough to pay off a two-million-dollar debt by the weekend. He began to tear Troy's home office apart, looking for *anything* that might tell him where Troy had hidden a large sum of money. What would happen if he couldn't find it?

When the door opened and Dave stood there, Aaron was in a sweat. His heart was beating so fast, he didn't know what to do. He couldn't even run to him, welcome him home. All he could think about was this money. Should he confess what was happening to Dave? If he did that, he'd have to tell him he wasn't Troy. No, he could never do that.

"I came home early. Wanted to surprise you. What's going on?" Dave asked.

"Ah, nothing, ah, welcome home. Sorry, I'm looking for something, that's all. Just get here?"

"Yeah. Was that the phone?"

"Oh, yeah, ah . . . just Darren . . . something about work, you know him."

Dave's gaze took in the turned over drawers and

disarrayed closet. "It's a funny time to call."

"You know Darren."

"Troy, what's wrong?" Dave walked into the room. "You look like you're going to have a heart attack."

"I lost something. I mean I put it somewhere and . . ." He couldn't go on. He was shaking like a leaf.

Dave placed both hands on his shoulders. "Calm down. Just think about the last place you saw it."

"That's it, I didn't see it. I've never seen it. I know nothing about it."

"What is it?"

"Two million dollars." Troy sank down on the edge of the desk chair, head in his hands. He shook his head. "Two fucking million."

"Two million dollars?" Dave echoed. "Jesus Christ. Where did you get two million dollars?"

Aaron glanced at him, trying not to let this situation drown him. "The um . . . company, I was keeping it safe for my father. We need it now and I can't remember where I put it."

"Usually, you put that kind of cash in the bank . . . unless . . . shit, Troy, is your dad cheating the IRS?"

If only it was that.

"No, it's a huge, ah, purchase."

"Two million dollars?"

It was clear Dave didn't believe him. He wasn't a fool. "Listen, never mind. I have to find it." Aaron stood. "Any idea where Troy . . . I mean . . . where I stash stuff?"

Dave gave him a strange look. "I . . . well . . . did you put it in the safety deposit box at the bank?"

"I have a . . . yeah . . . right, maybe. The safety deposit box. Do you know where the key is?"

"How would I know? It's your safety deposit box, not mine. What's going on with you? You are always so organized. It's not like you to forget where you put stuff."

"Look, don't lecture me. Just help me look, okay?"

"Sure, although this discussion isn't over. Something doesn't smell right here, Troy."

"Okay, we'll talk later," Aaron said, pulling out another drawer and dumping the contents on the bed.

Dave found the key to a safety deposit box in Troy's junk box. It was sitting on the top shelf in the closet. It was in an envelope with the name of the bank written on it. He stared at it for a moment. Troy had opened a safety deposit box at the bank after they'd been robbed two years ago. He said it was for his 'important documents.' The subject of two million dollars, however, had never come up before, and Dave wondered just what Darren had gotten Troy into. "I found it," he called out.

Troy came running. He threw his arms around him and hugged him. "You've just saved my life." He took the key, read what was written on the envelope and raced across the room. "What time does the bank open?"

"Nine o'clock. Same as all banks. Troy, I'm really worried about you."

"Great." He turned around, smiled. "Go eat some breakfast. Glad you're back, sweetie."

"Troy, we need to talk about this. This is a hell of a lot of money. What's it for? Where did it come from?"

"It's okay, all good," he said. He pecked Dave on the cheek. "Going to shower. Be down to join you in a minute."

Dave stood there in the middle of the floor for a long time before he could convince himself to move. He didn't like this. He didn't like it one bit.

Downstairs, Manuela prepared breakfast. The smell of bacon and eggs called to him and Dave walked slowly toward the dining room like a zombie. He was suffering from jet lag big time. This was not how he'd envisioned his homecoming.

He sat drinking coffee, reflecting on Troy's agitation. At least he hadn't caught him with another man. He wasn't sure which was worse, Troy cheating or Troy in a financial bind. He waited for his husband to join him, his stomach growling. Manuela came out into the dining room and glanced at him. "You ready, señor?"

"I'm waiting for Troy so that we can breakfast together."

"Señor Troy has already left," she said.

Dave narrowed his eyes. "Really?"

"Si, señor," she said. "I saw him drive away a few minutes ago."

Dave got up and went outside. Troy's car was gone. What the hell was going on? Troy had seemed so stressed out this morning, just like his good old self. He'd never seen him quite so rattled, even when Darren got on his case. Why would Troy be holding onto money like that? It didn't make any sense. No sense at all.

Dave thanked Manuela for the breakfast and went out to his car. He was going to take a swing by and talk to Darren this morning before he went to work.

Aaron sat in a little café on the ground floor of an office building across the street from the Wells Fargo twin towers on South Grand, waiting anxiously for the bank to open. He drummed his fingers on the table, thinking that if he didn't get into that bank soon, he was going to have a breakdown. Homeless people, hands outstretched, begging for change, shuffled back and forth between well-heeled office workers hurrying to their offices in the heart of the city's financial district.

I might be out here with my begging cup one day. I can't believe this is happening to me . . . He'd left one nightmare just to be plunged into another one.

He nodded and mouthed *thanks* as the waiter held up a

coffee pot for a refill, just as his cell phone rang. It said, *unknown caller*. He flipped it open and put it to his ear.

"Hey, Troy. Walter Berman here."

Aaron hadn't spoken to the man since they'd had lunch with Matt. Before Aaron could respond, Berman said, "Looks like your buddy Matt bought everything, lock, stock and barrel. We're transferring the funds as we speak. His grandmother must have been loaded with that kind of money. So, everything is in place. You're home free. No one will ever find it now, except you of course, fully laundered. I took my ten percent."

"I don't know what you're . . ." Aaron shook his head. "What do you mean . . . what about the global development company and the . . ." He trailed off.

"You're a real funny guy, Troy," he laughed. "Have a nice life." The man hung up.

Aaron swallowed. He stared at the phone then looked across the street. The bank was open. He threw down a couple of bills beside the coffee cup and hightailed it across the road, fingering the key in his hand.

He felt bad ducking out on Dave this morning, but he really couldn't handle any more questions, questions he didn't have any answers to.

Aaron had a sick feeling in the pit of his stomach as the teller pointed him toward a bank of elevators. Another teller met him and led him to a long, gleaming annex room. After checking his ID, the teller took him all the way into the back to his brother's safety deposit box. She told him to holler if he needed anything and then left him alone.

Had Troy stolen money from his best friend? Shit, could he have stooped any lower? Aaron ran his sweaty fingers against his pants, then over the box. He inserted the key and lifted the cover. What kind of a monster . . . He paused, swallowing hard. There right on top was a photograph, one of those that you took in a photo booth at a shopping mall.

Two small boys, identical to one another, sat cuddled against a woman, a pretty blonde with beautiful blue eyes. At first, Aaron didn't recognize the woman. Who was she? She was smiling and beautiful and . . .

Mother.

The woman in the photograph was his mother and she was hugging her sons . . . Aaron and Troy.

Tears sprang to his eyes. They couldn't have been more than two years old, probably just before they were separated. Troy had kept this photograph here in a place he knew it would always be safe.

There was an envelope. In it were old letters. He turned the envelope upside down and something went clunk into the box. *Troy's wedding band.*

Aaron picked it up and looked at it. A simple gold band with an inscription . . . he was lucky that Dave hadn't brought up the subject again. Aaron slipped it on his finger. It fit perfectly. It felt right.

He studied the letters. They were written to Darren from his mother, desperately pleading with him to come home. *She loved the son of a bitch.* She promised to be whatever he wanted . . . she promised to sell her soul. Her last one asked him why he didn't write. "Don't you love me at all? How is Troy? I miss him."

Aaron folded it in two. He was about to put everything away when he found another envelope right at the back. This one was new. It said 'Dave.'

He felt guilty taking it out and unfolding it but he had to know.

My beautiful, darling David,

If you are reading this, it is because they've found my body. As everything I have is yours, I knew eventually you'd come here. I can't explain why I did what I did, and there's no way out now. I got lost. Maybe I was always lost.

I had to leave to protect you. I couldn't stand the thought of anyone hurting you and they would have to, to get to me. God, Dave, you are the only one I've ever loved, even if I hurt you again and again. Sometimes the power of how much I loved you scared me, and I'd try to hide. Sex with other men was my way to do that, I guess. None of those men meant anything to me. And you must believe me when I say you were constantly in my head when I was with someone else. I've hurt so many people.

There's so much you don't know. I leave you my ring because it is the most precious thing in the world to me, and I didn't want it to be forever lost . . . in case . . . Know that I loved you the best I could . . . but never good enough.

Yours always, my beautiful love. My heart, my body and my very soul,
Troy

Aaron felt strange reading the letter. His first instinct was to rip it up and throw it across the room. It enraged him.

Oh God, I'm losing my mind.

He felt like David was his now, and yet, he wasn't. He'd never been his. All of Dave's feelings were for another man, his brother Troy. Christ, and there was no money here. There was no money in the safety deposit box. Only more questions.

Mobsters, swindling money, cheating on Dave, poisoning neighbors' trees . . . Was it possible that Troy had been mentally ill? What had it been like, being raised by Darren? Aaron had always thought that he'd had the worst of it, an alcoholic mother, but maybe he'd gotten off easy.

How could he feel sympathy for Troy if he'd stolen money from his best friend, if he was involved with drug dealers?

And was he still alive? There was no evidence that Troy was dead, only the idea that Troy felt his life was threatened.

He'd left this life to protect Dave. Somehow Aaron believed that Troy loved Dave. Hell, he could be living the good life somewhere in some foreign country spending Matt's inheritance and hiding money belonging to mobsters. And what if he came back? What if suddenly his intense love for Dave compelled him to show up on the doorstep?

Aaron left the bank. He sat in his car a long time. He had worse troubles. There was two million dollars missing, money owed to a mobster who'd murder him and ask questions later. And there was Matt, poor Matt, who'd just been milked out of a shitload of money. How in the hell was Aaron supposed to explain that?

Going to the police was not an option. Thanks to Troy, he was into this up to his neck. He had no idea what in hell he was going to do. He took out the photograph of his mother, her arms around two little boys that had no idea that soon they'd be parted forever. He pressed it to his chest and wondered if he should do the same as Troy had.

Run.

Darren was looking over some papers when David walked into his office. He looked up in surprise. "Well, hello my boy. This is a nice surprise. What are you doing here?"

"We need to talk."

"Talk away."

Dave closed the door. He walked over to the desk and placed his palms down, meeting Darren's gaze. "What's going on? Are you in trouble, the company?"

"Why would you ask that?" He sat back in his seat.

"What is this about two million dollars?"

"Troy tell you that?" He lifted an eyebrow.

"Two million dollars, Darren!"

"Okay, right, it's a loan. It was to be put away for safe

keeping." He stood.

"That's bullshit. Try again." Dave folded his arms across his chest, waited.

"You have no business in this, David, stay out of it."

"I'm in it. It involves Troy. He's freaking out." David lowered his voice. "I know who you went to the last time the company was in hawk. I'm not an idiot, Darren."

"It's a favor."

"It's the fucking mob! One wrong move and you and Troy will end up in the middle of the river. I know you have no respect for Troy. He might have been a good man if you hadn't fucked with his head. I deal with the damage you caused him every fucking day. But I'll tell you one thing," David pointed his finger at him, "I won't stand by and watch you get him killed."

"David, you're a nice man. I'm glad Troy has you in his life to calm him down but you're in his life because I allow you to be. Don't forget that."

David's eyes widened. "Fuck you, Darren. Just fuck you! You don't control me."

"One word from me and that little coward would leave you flat and you know it! I own him. He'll do what I tell him to do."

"Oh no," David said, "not this time, Darren."

"David," Darren barked as David got to the door, "stay out of the way or you're going to get hurt."

"Is that a threat?" David glanced at him, hand on the door.

"No, boy, that's a promise."

CHAPTER THIRTEEN

Aaron sat in his car, unsure of what to do next. How in hell did he get himself out of this mess? The last time he'd been in trouble he'd reached out to his twin . . . who really did a number on him. He cranked up the engine. He needed gas. It surprised him that he hadn't thought about it sooner, but the car was a hybrid and he'd only had to fill it up once since he'd been in LA.

He drove around downtown, his thoughts spiraling as he hunted for a gas station. The incredible buildings commanding the skyline spoke of money that Skid Row, just two blocks from the Wells Fargo building, belied. He found a gas station and an eager kid approached him as he pulled up to the pump.

"Sir, we're doing a fundraiser for our school. Two dollars to wash your car?"

It was the last thing the car needed . . . but then again, Aaron needed time to think, to come up with something other than blank terror, so he agreed to let the school kids wash the car.

One of the older ones put Armor All on his tires after three of them washed it by hand. The teenager was kneeling on the ground and suddenly turned to Aaron, a troubled look on his face.

He approached Aaron who seemed to be the only one aware of the hostile expressions on the faces of the drivers waiting to get their vehicles washed.

"I know you're married," the teen said to him, indicating Aaron's left hand. Aaron had forgotten he'd left the bank wearing the ring.

"Yes, why?" Aaron said, wondering where the kid was

going with this.

"Well, it's none of my business but I wasn't sure if you knew you have a tracking device right near the wheel hub."

Aaron gaped at him. "Are you sure?"

"Yeah. It's not a sophisticated one, but in case your wife's having you followed, I thought you'd want to know."

Aaron felt the sweat start under his armpits and move down his spine.

"Can you get it for me? I'll give you twenty dollars."

The kid held out his hand. Aaron gave him the cash and the kid trotted back to the car, reached around the tire and pretending to wipe it with a rag, took his hand away and came back, a small black box in his hand.

"Thanks." Aaron put it into his jacket pocket. How long had it been on there? He had no idea what to do next, but he knew he could no longer do this alone. He paid the kids well for their efforts then drove to Matt's office building.

It was time to start coming clean. He just hoped that Matt wasn't a violent man.

Matt was in a meeting when Aaron got to his office. His assistant wouldn't even put a call through to him, but Aaron was so badly shaken she seemed to realize the situation was urgent.

"Is it . . . personal?" she asked him as he hovered over her desk.

"A matter of life or death." His voice cracked and his hand shook as he wiped the perspiration from his lip. His heart was racing. He had a strange taste in his mouth and wondered if he was having a heart attack.

"Troy?"

He turned a few seconds later and found Matt hurrying out of his office toward him.

"What's wrong?"

"We need to talk."

Matt said nothing for a moment then took him by the arm and led him to a conference room.

"Hold all my calls," he told his assistant.

Inside the room, he turned on the lights. Aaron noticed dead floral bouquets and dispirited looking pot plants bunched on one end.

"Take a seat." Matt pointed to the clean end. "I'm going to give you a little cognac. I think you're in shock."

God . . . he is being so nice to me. Aaron sat, his hands slippery on the leather arms of his chair. He took the drink when Matt handed him the glass and downed it.

Better. In spite of the fire in his throat.

"What the fuck is going on?" Matt asked.

"You need to sit down."

"I am sitting down."

Aaron glanced at him. "Oh." He stared into his glass. The cognac had warmed him slightly. He really wanted another shot but getting blotto wouldn't help.

"I don't know where to start, Matt, except to say I am so fucking sorry for what my brother's done to you."

"Your brother?"

"Troy."

"But you're Troy."

"No. I'm his twin, Aaron. He . . . offered to help me out of a jam a few months ago by taking his place."

"Oh, for fuck's sake, Troy. I've heard you tell some wild tales in the time I've known you—"

"It's true. And until this morning I had no idea he was conning you. Look, there is so much I need to explain but the bottom line is this. I have no idea how much you gave my brother and his pal Walter Berman, but Berman called me this morning thinking I'm Troy. He told me you'd transferred the money to him and he in turn put it into another account. They've stolen your money. Everything you've been doing here is . . . well, I guess, it isn't real."

"Isn't real? Are you fucking shitting me?"

Aaron shook his head slowly. Matt flew across the table at him, attacking him. Aaron didn't blame him, but he fought back as Matt's fist connected with his jaw. The man had a right hook on him that would have dropped a heavyweight.

"Everyone said you were a phony and I didn't listen. I trusted you!"

"I'm sorry. It wasn't me."

"Stop with the fucking bullshit!" Matt pinned him to the floor, laying more punches on him. Aaron fought back, but he was no match for the brute strength of Matt.

The man's fist connected with Aaron's jaw one last time and then the world turned black.

When Aaron awoke, Matt and another man were sitting in the conference room, talking. It took Aaron a few seconds to realize he was sitting in a chair beside them, his hands and legs strapped to his seat with masking tape. The man talking to Matt was Patrick and they glared at him.

"He's awake," Patrick said.

Shit. I wish I was dead. Aaron's head ached, his left eye throbbed and his two previously broken fingers felt like they'd been snapped in two. He tasted blood on his lips. It was awful.

"We've contacted the police. They're on their way. The office address we had for Walter Berman was actually his apartment. They just arrested him. He took out a pretty big chunk of money, but . . ." Matt paused and glanced at Patrick before proceeding, "he's confessed that you and he swindled me."

"I'm telling you, it wasn't me."

"Ah, yes. The elusive twin." Matt spat the words out. "I've known you for a long time and you've told me some whoppers, but there *is no twin.*"

"Yes, there is. Ask my father. He'll tell you." Aaron felt light-headed. "We were separated when we were about two. I got our mom, Troy got our father." Aaron was in agony. He kept seeing spots before his eyes.

Patrick slid something across the small space between him and Matt on the conference room table. From this angle, Aaron could see it was the photo of him and Troy and their mother.

"Holy fuck." Matt sat back in his chair. He glanced at Aaron. "This is you?" He stuck out his bottom lip, as if deep in thought.

"This letter is for you. It's been opened." Patrick slid an envelope across the table to . . . Dave.

"Oh, my God." Aaron's voice croaked.

"Twins, you've got a fucking *twin?*" Dave shouted at him and tore open the letter. His eyes glazed with tears as he read the contents.

"You're the one I've been with the last month?"

Aaron hated the look on Dave's face. Sheer and utter revulsion.

"Yes."

"You bastard! I slept with you. I don't even know you. You fucking scumbag!"

"I love you!"

"Don't you talk to me about love. You know nothing about it!"

"Yes, I do." Aaron choked on his own tears as Dave leaned across him and yanked the wedding ring off his finger.

"This isn't yours to wear. Where is Troy?"

"I don't know."

Matt hauled off and hit Aaron so hard, blood spurted from

his nose and mouth.

"For God's sake!" Patrick stood and pulled Matt off him. "Jesus Christ, Matt. If he hadn't come in here and told you about the ruse, you'd have lost everything!"

"I don't have it back yet!"

"You will. They've put a trace on the money." Patrick paused. "Aaron . . . are you okay? You don't look so good."

Aaron was too weak to respond. His jaw wouldn't work. Broken. His head lolled forward, blood dripping from his mouth.

Dave spoke to him, but Aaron couldn't talk. He was aware of toppling forward, taking the chair with him . . .

Dave called an ambulance. It was obvious once Aaron was in the emergency room of the Good Samaritan Hospital that Aaron had been telling the truth. Their x-rays of his jaw showed that he had none of the titanium implants that filled Troy's mouth.

Where the hell was Troy?

When Darren Mayer stormed into the hallway of the emergency room, he didn't look pleased to see Dave. He looked even less pleased to know that his son Aaron was undergoing surgery.

"I don't give a fuck about that little runt. I stopped thinking about that little asshole a long time ago."

Asshole? Aaron was everything Troy was not . . . No. Aaron was a liar. Just like Troy. Only . . . nicer.

"Where is Troy?" Darren thundered. "That little bastard stole the money. He was supposed to deliver it Saturday. Fuck!"

He kicked the wall. A security guard ambled over, hand on his holstered gun.

"Settle down, sir."

"Fuck you, you goddam rent-a-cop." Darren turned on Dave, his rage in full bloom.

"Thanks to Troy the mob's gonna be after us. I'm gettin' outta town. I suggest you leave that piece of shit in here to fend for himself. You need to disappear, too."

He left the hospital, the security guard shaking his head. Dave said nothing. He sat in one of the chairs in the waiting room, eyeing the ancient, half-torn copies of *People* and *Time* magazines.

Dave didn't know what to think. He'd torn the letter from Troy to shreds. In his heart of hearts, he'd known something was off from the moment 'Troy' had started making nice with the neighbors and being so sweet to him. No. He knew for certain when 'Troy' had cooked for him.

He tried not to think about how spectacular the sex had been with . . . Aaron. The truth was, he'd fallen for the new and definitely improved Troy. He had to stop thinking of him as Troy and think of him as Aaron. He began to pace. His cell phone rang. Matt.

Dave took the call outside. It was a blustery day and the wind blew dust particles into his mouth and eyes.

"The cops were here," Matt said. He sounded a lot calmer. "My bank tells me I'll be able to recover all the money."

There was a moment of silence.

"Do you have any idea where it was transferred to?" Dave asked.

"They won't tell me, but they do say that Troy just tried to go into a bank . . . in Mexico to take out the funds. He couldn't access it online. Guess he's desperate because he didn't realize the account had been flagged."

"Troy. Is. In. Mexico?" Dave's emotions roller coasted. The bastard. *The utter, fucking bastard.*

"They just arrested him but I'm not sure if they'll extradite him. You know there's no treaty between the US and

Mexico ... they've been known to cooperate in homicide cases, but this involves money. They've arrested him but that's all I know."

Dave was relieved that Matt's money was safe. The man never once asked if Aaron was okay. Really, it had been so brave of Aaron to walk into Matt's office and admit the truth.

"We found a tracer in Aaron's pocket," Matt said. "There's a SIM card. We tracked it to somebody called Joe Carson."

"Joe from Troy's office?"

"Yeah! The police spoke to him. Looks like he had nothing to do with the finances. He believed he'd been tracking Troy's car. Apparently, he's in love with Troy."

"He has a way with people."

"What about the two mil?" Matt asked.

"No idea. I'm still waiting to talk to Aaron."

Matt snorted. "I wouldn't even bother."

Geez, Matt was pissed at Aaron. They ended the call on that note.

Dave checked his messages. A few of his clients wanted to re-arrange appointments. He was happy to do that. He pushed off all his training sessions for the following day. He walked back into the hospital waiting room. He kept remembering how pitiful the battered Aaron had looked strapped to Matt's office chair.

Aaron had saved Matt's fortune and deserved his thanks, not a brutal beating. He had no idea how long he sat there, but he felt a hand on his shoulder.

"Your friend is awake. I think he'd like to talk to you," one of the nurses told him. The emergency room was filled with indigent people. Dave passed a young woman whose arms and legs were covered in needle tracks and a young man in a wheelchair who was talking to himself.

Aaron was sitting in a hospital bed in a semi-private room. An old man lay next to him, sleeping. The nurse drew a curtain around Aaron's bed to give them a little privacy.

"I'm sorry," Aaron said. His lips and eyes looked puffy.

"You should be." Dave sat beside him. Aaron seemed to be having difficulty swallowing. The nurse held an ice chip to his lips with a paper towel. He sucked and moaned.

"There are plenty here. If he needs more, just shake one out, but no liquids just yet," she told Dave.

Dave nodded. He had no intention of taking care of Aaron. He wanted to know why the fuck the man had done this to him. Replaced Troy . . . seduced him.

"Explain yourself," he said as soon as they were alone.

Aaron's eyes remained half closed.

"I was in trouble. Troy said he'd help me. He told me to meet him."

"Trouble seems to follow you both." Dave couldn't hide the disdain in his voice. "What kind of trouble?"

"I owed money to a loan shark. They came after me. Broke my fingers." Aaron seemed to have trouble swallowing again. Dave sighed. He shook an ice cube out of the plastic cup on the bed tray and ran it across Aaron's parched lips.

"That's why you had the cast when I came home that first night. That was when you made the switch?"

"Yes."

"Why? Why'd you do it?"

"I hadn't seen him in a long time. He didn't even call when Mother died. I took care of her for a long time. She was a drunk. She gambled. I paid off her debts."

He shifted on the bed, obviously in pain.

"You borrowed money to pay off her debts and then couldn't pay it back?"

"Right."

"What do you do for a living?"

"Landscaping." Aaron's eyes drifted shut. The nurse came back to the bed.

"He's in a lot of pain. The morphine releases into his system automatically. He won't be coherent again for a while. Come back in the morning."

Fuck. He wanted to know more. He was so damned mad at Troy. And Aaron. He started to feel a little sorry for Aaron. He was beginning to see that Troy had duped him too. Probably told him he'd have a nice, easy life as Troy . . . *Oh, boy.* When he thought of all the problems Troy had created around their lives, with their friends and neighbors. And now . . . the mob.

Shit. Maybe Darren was right and he should get out of Dodge. He stood and walked out of the room, not even looking back at the broken man in the bed. He'd been prepared to leave Troy when he came home, why did he want to keep Aaron around?

Troy Mayer couldn't believe he was in a jail cell.

How the fuck had they traced him all the way to Juárez?

The guy in the cell next to him was banging on the wall. He'd been at it for hours. Troy felt only slight fear about being in here. Cereso Prison was for drug smugglers. He was only guilty of trying to get money from his bank account.

Walter Berman had sure fucked up. Troy blamed himself for not staying in touch with the guy. He really thought he'd had all his bases covered. He leaned back against the stone wall, wondering how much everyone back in the States knew. He thought about the hot young man waiting for him back at the house. He and Juan-Manuel had been having so much fun. He'd hardly thought about his life back in LA and never, ever, thought about Dave.

Because it hurt too much. He loved Dave . . . but love was a bad deal. Love sucked. He'd never trusted anyone. Never would.

Except Dave. Damn. I can't even call him . . .

He listened as the man next door stopped banging on the wall. One of the prison guards was walking through. Someone was being released. He craned forward as footsteps clattered on the hard floor outside the cell.

They stopped next door. An exchange in Spanish.

"*Finalmente!*" a gruff voice shouted.

More footsteps. The prison guard looked into Troy's cell.

He'd contacted his attorney thanks to Juan-Manuel who'd gone to the bank with him.

When Troy had been ambushed, he'd muttered one word to his lover. "Teléfono." Juan-Manuel had nodded and slipped out of the bank. He had planned for this contingency when they'd left for the bank. With so much money involved in the transfer and so much at stake, he'd been right to be worried . . . but damned stupid and foolish to have walked in there when he couldn't electronically access the funds.

His only hope was Juan-Manuel making the call. Troy's attorney in Tijuana had a huge retainer and would act quickly if he wanted the rest of the promised cash. Yes, he trusted Juan-Manuel to come through for him. Troy expected to be out in the morning, but still, this was too much restriction for his comfort.

He tried to think ahead, what needed to happen next. He had to get the money he'd stashed on the boat. He'd been stupid to leave the damned thing in Morro Bay, but he couldn't risk the hidden cash being found. Three days until Saturday. Plenty of time for him to get back to Cali, get the boat and be on his way.

Troy closed his eyes, imagining himself on the beach at Aruba. Ah, yes, he could almost feel the sun's warmth now. He was good at imagining things. He heard a dripping sound.

Come on, block it out. Nothing drips on the beach at Aruba. He put himself back in the zone. A tropical drink in his hand, a hot, hung guy lying beside him.

Which one?

The dripping sound intensified. Rain. It was fucking raining! In his cell! All the weeks he'd been tooling around Mexico he hadn't encountered rain. He cursed himself for venturing away from his coastal hacienda to go to the bank. *I should have waited.*

Footsteps. The guard returned and gave him a toothy smile, the kind only large sums of cash could produce in some people.

Troy stood, working hard to hide his anxiety. He walked past the row of men staring at him. Two other Americans picked up on drug charges right before Troy had been talking loudly all afternoon. They were pacing their cell.

"Call the American Embassy!" one of them shouted through the bars at Troy.

Yeah, right. He nodded though, because condemned men needed to have some hope, and because he was in a good mood thanks to his early release. Dusk kissed the sky outside as he glanced around the police station. No sign of Juan-Manuel, or his attorney. That was weird.

The desk sergeant waved him over and in rapid Spanish spiced heavily with local jargon, basically told him to get the hell out of Mexico. Troy retrieved his wallet and the key guard to his gated house. His wallet had been stripped of its cash, but his Mexican driver's license and credit cards were still in it.

He stepped outside.

"Hey, big boy."

A hooker winked at him. He didn't register a single thing. The last thing he wanted to do was get picked up again for . . . *anything.* He turned to his right and kept walking. What in the hell was going on? Had his attorney bailed him out? Yes . . . it had to have been him. He walked quickly, hugging the walls of the colorful buildings he passed. This was a dangerous town at night, and he didn't want to be out on the street. He stopped several times and checked over his shoulder, but nobody was following him.

He detoured and backtracked several times until about two hours later, he reached his house. Lights blazed but he studied it from across the road for several minutes. No sign of movement inside. He ran over to the big iron gate, swiped the key card and went inside. He closed the gate again, checking up and down the street. The silence was eerie.

Past the leafy courtyard, he moved through the front door which was closed, but not locked. He walked down the hallway and looked into all the rooms. The place had been tossed, his computer was gone, and his emergency cash supply had vanished from the can of Ajax under the sink. He almost couldn't believe Juan-Manuel had done this. Well, he'd been right not to trust the little dickhead.

He went upstairs, relieved when his secret safe appeared untouched. He opened it, the tension dropping from his shoulders as he retrieved several wads of cash, his expensive fake passport, iPad, spare boat keys and a pay-as-you-go, untraceable cell phone.

In his bedroom, he went to take a backpack out of the closet when he realized somebody was in the bed.

A pair of high heels peeked out from the sheets. He shook his head, walked over and touched a slim, brown leg.

"Nancy." It was a statement, not a question. She giggled, turning over to face him.

"I've been waiting forever," she said. She reached for him, pulling him down to the bed. "They know everything," she said. "Except for where the money is. I've left Darren."

Her mouth clamped down on Troy's, leaving him breathless.

"We don't need to hide anymore," she said, her naked body draping over Troy's.

For a long moment, he let her kiss and hug him, but she was not on his mind. In fact, he never expected to see her again. She'd been reporting to him on his husband and brother's activities. He thought he'd be long gone by the time she came looking for him.

A minor calamity. The bigger one was the fucking boat. Aaron hadn't been near it since the day Troy had lured him there. What if he decided to go back to Morro Bay for it?

He tried to push Nancy off him, but she would have none of it. He gave himself up to her sensual seduction. There would be time to get rid of her.

Plenty of time . . .

CHAPTER FOURTEEN

Aaron awoke rather violently. Somebody was shaking him. His eyes opened. Dave. He would have smiled except that his mouth wouldn't move.

"Wake up! I want a word with you."

Aaron was so pleased to see Dave he let the man shove him around a moment.

"Why did you switch places with Troy?"

"What time is it?" Aaron finally managed.

"Eight o'clock in the morning. Now answer the question."

"Water. Please."

Dave sighed in an exaggerated way and left the bed. He returned a few minutes later with what looked like a child's sippy cup. He could tell by the condensation that it was iced. Dave rather nastily shoved a straw into the cup then inserted it into Aaron's mouth. Sucking was hard.

"He's not supposed to suck," the nurse chided Dave as she came into the curtained space. "You'll hurt him." She elbowed Dave aside. Dave shot Aaron a guilty look, then sat down, watching the nurse help Aaron into a sitting position. She held the cup for him as he drank. She popped some pillows behind him then left them alone.

"Well, I could make some comment about the sucking, but I won't. Okay, I'm waiting for an answer." Dave barked.

Aaron sank back against the pillows, longing for more water. The nurse returned with a small bottle, twisted off the cap and handed it to him.

"I'll bring you some soup in about an hour," she said.

Aaron drank deeply. He felt a little better already. Whatever the hell drugs he'd been on had produced horrible dreams and a morning fogginess.

"I'm waiting, Aaron."

"He said he would help me." God . . . this is a nightmare. This is really happening . . .

"When was this?"

"A few days before I met you at the house . . . when I had the broken fingers."

"Go on."

It took all his strength to talk. "He called me. Out of the blue. I didn't know why. But I was scared. I was hiding from the loan sharks."

"Where were you?"

"Los Osos."

"Where is that?"

"Up the coast. Near Morro Bay."

"Go on."

Aaron turned his head with difficulty and stared at the handsome man he loved. Dave looked awful. He didn't look like he'd had any sleep.

"I'm sorry." Aaron's words came out hoarsely.

"Go on."

"I told him I was in trouble. I had to get out of my house. The sharks torched my car. I slept in the forest then went to meet him in the morning at his boat."

"He doesn't have a boat." Dave's tone was sharp.

"Yes, he does. It's called The Promise."

Dave looked skeptical but said nothing.

"A friend of mine gave me a ride and I took the bus to Morro Bay and when I got on the boat I was alone. Troy had left a note, telling me I should take his place. He said I deserved a turn at having things."

"Yes. I saw the note."

"You did?"

Dave nodded. "He never said anything about me?"

"He never said anything about . . . anything. I walked into

a bear trap the second I arrived at your house. The neighbors accosted me." Aaron closed his eyes. "My brother is a total shithead. I've been through hell. The only nice thing was meeting you and getting to make some awesome people feel better about ever having met Troy Mayer."

There was a moment of silence.

"You lied to me."

"Yes." No denying it.

Another pause.

"They say you will be leaving today. They need the bed. I'll take you home, but you and I . . . we're through. You can pack your stuff and move out. I'm selling the house. Since you are not married to me, you have no say in the decision."

Aaron closed his eyes. Tears leaked from the lids, but his arms felt like lead. He couldn't do anything to stop them flowing.

"I never lied about my feelings for you," he said. "Never. I've never . . . I've never been with a man before and I love you."

Silence. When he opened his teary eyes, Aaron saw that he was alone.

Where in the hell do I go from here? Who in hell can I love after loving someone like Dave?

Dave returned to the hospital at two and found Aaron more or less mobile. The guy looked pitiful with his distended jaw, broken shoulder on one side and broken hand on the other. He walked with a halting step. The doctor said he had two broken ribs.

I can't send him packing in this state. He can spend the night . . . then he's out tomorrow.

Aaron thanked him for picking him up then fell asleep in the car. He slept all the way to Bel Air.

"Is Mr. Mayer okay?" the gate guard asked, looking

alarmed.

"He had a car accident. He's recovering."

Where was Troy's car, anyway? He'd have to ask Aaron when he was awake. At the house, he woke Aaron, but had to help the guy out of the car. The gardener came running. Inside the house, Manuela cried. Nikko Watanabe called the house phone. Everyone was concerned for 'Troy's' well-being. For now, Dave would call him Troy, too, and in a couple of days, would quietly let them all know that he had finally dumped his lousy husband.

Alberto helped Dave get Aaron up the stairs and into the bedroom. Aaron sat on the edge of the bed. Alberto made himself scarce as Dave took off Aaron's shoes and socks.

"I'm going to call you Troy until you leave this house. I don't want any confusion with the people around us. Understood?"

Aaron nodded.

"You can stay tonight. It's obvious you're in no shape to drive, but tomorrow, you're out of here."

"Okay."

"Where is Troy's car?" Dave looked at him.

"Matt's office building."

"Okay. Right. You drove there yesterday. It must still be there." He sat back on his haunches. "Where is the boat?"

"Don't know." Aaron wobbled unsteadily. Dave felt a little guilty. The guy wasn't leaning against anything.

Dave took off Aaron's pants, leaving his underwear and T-shirt on him and pressed him down against the unmade bed. How weird that Manuela had left it this way.

He would say something to her, but for now, Dave still had questions.

"What do you mean you don't know where the boat is? Where did you leave it?"

"Morro Bay. I drove Troy's car back from there. I know

nothing about boats. It should still be there."

"You remember the slip number?"

Aaron lay back, blinking. "Seventeen." He looked pale.

"Want some pills? They gave you a ton of them."

"Got anything for a broken heart?" Aaron asked.

"No. That I can't help you with."

Aaron closed his eyes. His steady breathing told Dave that he was asleep. Down in the kitchen, he heard voices.

"Jesus Christ!"

Manuela jumped back in fright as Dave walked into the room. She flushed crimson.

"Troy?"

Dave rounded the kitchen island and saw the man he'd married hesitate as he prepared to leap out of the kitchen window like a common thief.

"Don't you fucking dare," Dave ground out. "You stay here and face me like a man."

Manuela began to wring her hands, sobbing. "He has a gun. I give him money."

Dave gaped at her. The distraction was all Troy needed to vanish out of the window. Dave heard him dropping like a sack of potatoes on the other side. He couldn't believe that Troy had come back here . . . and now he wouldn't even face Dave, after everything he'd done. Dave ran to the front door and flung it open in time to see Troy racing off in his car. How the hell had he found it?

He stood, trying to gather his thoughts. He pulled his cell phone from his pants pocket and called Matt.

"Troy's here," he said without any preamble when Matt answered.

"Here, where?"

"He just came to the house. He's gone again. He was in his car . . . how the hell did he get it? Aaron said he left it at your office building."

"His dear mama came for it," Matt said.

"Who?"

"Nancy . . . you know, Darren's new wife."

Dave was stunned. The shocks kept coming. How had she known where it was?

"She bailed him out of jail. She tells me they're running off together," Matt said. "She's damned lucky I don't slug women, or another member of the Mayer family would be laid up in the emergency room."

He hung up on Dave who glanced up and down the street, then closed the front door, stepping back inside. He'd always known Troy was a rat-bastard the first time he caught him in bed with another man. Troy hadn't seemed upset, just pissed that he'd been caught. Oh, he'd said all the right things, just without a note of sincerity. Dave knew that now. He'd just seen the same look on the man's face when he'd caught him in the kitchen.

Dave retraced his steps and found Manuela sobbing as she swept the kitchen floor. She was so obviously distraught that he felt compelled to put his arms around her. He asked her what had happened. She told him Troy had appeared inside the laundry room.

"He told me he wanted money. I give him twenty dollars."

"That's all he got?"

She shook her head. "No. He had money hidden. He sent me to get my purse and I saw him taking the gun and the cash." She pointed to an air vent. The grill had been removed from it.

"Was there a lot?"

She shrugged. "He still took my twenty."

Dave took his wallet out, handed her a twenty-dollar bill and suggested she go home. She seemed relieved. She removed her apron, picked up her purse and left. He wondered if she would ever come back to the house again.

He called the security company that looked after the property. He asked them to come and change all the locks and to re-set the system with a new security code. It seemed a little like locking the stable door long after the horses had been ground into dog food, but it felt better than doing nothing. The house grew dark. He walked back upstairs to check on Aaron. He wouldn't have been surprised to find that he, too, had vanished but Aaron was in bed, asleep.

Switching on the lights, he came back to the kitchen and took some of Manuela's wonderful minestrone out of the freezer and defrosted it. He did a doubletake when Aaron came and stood in the doorway. He looked frail and so forlorn.

"Take a seat," Dave said.

"I had the weirdest dream." Aaron looked around the room. "I had a dream that Troy was in this house."

Dave sucked in a breath. "He was."

"Really?" Aaron seemed to sway. "Mind if I sit down?"

"Of course not. You . . . you've fucked me for Christ's sake. We're hardly strangers."

Aaron sat, a dejected air about him. "I've never felt him before. You know . . . that twin thing has never been strong for me. It was weird, though. It didn't feel good. It felt . . . black as night. I think I'm scared of my own brother."

"I think you have good reason to be. Guess who sprang him out of jail in Mexico and is now on the run with him?"

Aaron stared at him from his one good eye. "Who?"

"Nancy."

Aaron scrunched up his nose. "My father's wife?"

"Yeah." Dave realized Nancy was Aaron's stepmother, as well as Troy's.

"Eww . . . gross," Aaron said. For the first time in two days, Dave smiled faintly.

"Is he fucking her?"

"I assume."

"How could he? He's gay."

"He'd do it if it was to his advantage. Maybe he just holds his nose," Dave replied absently.

Aaron took an appreciative sniff. "Something smells good."

"Manuela made soup. There's also a loaf of garlic bread but I guess with your busted jaw that's not going to work."

"Right," Aaron said. "Do we have any wine?"

Dave opened a bottle of red wine and poured them each a glass. Aaron sat with him at the kitchen table. He ate two bowls of soup and sipped at his single glass of wine. He suddenly stopped. He'd clearly hit a wall.

"I'm going back to bed. Is that okay with you?"

"Of course."

"Sorry I'm not up to helping you clear the dishes."

"It's okay."

"I'm sorry for . . . everything."

"I know you are, Aaron. You said that."

"You really believe me?"

Dave nodded. "I don't think this has been much fun for you."

"You were. You were the best thing to ever happen to me." He got up from the table and left the kitchen.

Dave cleaned the kitchen, went upstairs and went to the other bedroom. He knew Aaron was a man of his word and would undoubtedly leave in the morning. But with what? He'd inherited some parts of Troy's life, but now both the life Aaron had once led and the life of riches that he'd glimpsed, were over.

In his bedroom, Dave had trouble sleeping. He switched on his laptop, surprised that he could access the Morro Bay marina online. They had a marina cam that took snapshots every thirty seconds. He called the harbor master and checked the online photos.

The Promise was still docked in slip number seventeen. He had a feeling Troy was heading back up to it. So what if he was? The man didn't want him. Dave certainly didn't want Troy anymore either. He bitterly regretted ever having met him.

He lay on his bed wondering if maybe Troy had hidden the two million dollars on the boat. Maybe he should tell Darren.

Dave called his father in law, who answered his cell phone on the second ring.

"David." Darren sounded terse. He was crying.

"I just got a call from the Hidden Hills Police Department. They found Troy's car wrapped around a telegraph pole. Nancy was in the passenger seat. They say she was dead before the impact even happened. She'd been shot in the head. They want me to identify her. Fuck! Why did he have to kill her?"

Darren Mayer sobbed like a nine-year-old girl. Dave wanted to hate him. And he did. But he also felt sorry for the guy. Troy had destroyed yet another life.

Troy reached his boat a little after two in the morning. He climbed aboard the vessel and found it was pretty much left the way he'd last seen it. He didn't want to make too much noise, so he climbed into the first bunk he could find, but hated the musty, salty smell to the crispy sheets and blankets. He was desperate to find the money he'd hidden on board, but it would have to wait until the morning.

He lay on the bed, passing a hand across his eyes. He could smell the gunshot residue on his skin and longed to take a shower. He'd have one as soon as he woke up, then he could set sail for the Caribbean.

Troy hadn't planned to sail alone but knew he wouldn't

stay that way for long. He had no trouble meeting new guys and would find one as soon as he could. He shuddered thinking about how he'd had to fuck Nancy.

Ugh. He needed that shower after all.

He took a quick one, but the chill inside him would not warm up.

Something's wrong . . .

No. He'd had to shoot Nancy. That was a necessity. It wasn't until he toweled off and lay back on the bed that he thought about the horrible fight they'd had. He had to shut the bitch up. She was a pain in the ass. When she told him she was pregnant . . . man, that was just too much. He'd gone bonkers.

He lay awake, letting night shadows bouncing off the marina lamps bother him more than they should. He fell asleep, convincing himself that he was in bed with Dave. That Dave loved him and wanted him . . . Dave fucking him . . . yum.

CHAPTER FIFTEEN

Aaron awoke feeling better than he had the day before. Thursday. Two days to go before the drug drop was due to take place Saturday. He knew Dave wanted him out and he didn't blame him. He got out of bed and took a shower, trying to keep his plastered shoulder and hand out of the spray. It wasn't easy considering they were not on the same limb.

He almost fell climbing out of the shower stall and let out a cry.

Dave came running in and caught him.

"What do you think you're doing?"

"Taking a shower."

"You're not ready for that."

"But I have to leave today."

"You can leave tomorrow. You don't even have transportation."

"Oh. Right. Yeah. I don't have a car."

"I would gladly let you keep Troy's but he took it. And, by the way, I want you to hear this from me, he killed Nancy."

Aaron almost fell again.

Dave led him back to bed. Just the nearness of the man gave Aaron an instant erection. He was so embarrassed, but Dave acted like he didn't notice it.

He covered Aaron with the bedclothes and said he'd come back with coffee.

Aaron lay in bed, wondering if Dave would really come back. The man gave off every sign of hating him. Not that he blamed him. He dressed himself as best he could, his skin still damp under his shirt.

"What are you doing?" Dave stood in the doorway, a tray in hand. The smell of coffee was so overwhelming, Aaron almost swooned. "You're in no shape to leave today. Get back into bed. Good God, Aaron. You're still wet."

Dave put the tray down on a chest of drawers and came to him.

"You're shivering." He peeled off the shirt. Aaron loved having the man so close to him, and yet, it was agonizing too, knowing all the things they'd done together and would never do again.

Dave grabbed a fresh towel and dabbed it onto Aaron's skin, drying him in a gentle way. He brought out an oversized sweater and put it on him.

"Get back into bed," he barked, ignoring Aaron's now rigid cock, which pointed at Dave's hip bone.

Aaron complied, allowing the man to cover him up once again.

Dave brought the tray to the bed and poured them each a cup of coffee.

"Look . . . I have no real . . . beef with you. I have to admit, the last month or so with you have been the best days of my whole married life. You gave me a glimpse of what could be," Dave said.

Aaron scooted up against the headboard, using his heels and ass to move into a sitting position. Dave reached behind him and plumped up an extra pillow for him.

"Thanks."

"And that's another thing." Dave frowned. "I should hate you because of that glimpse. This has been so wonderful, so . . . peaceful knowing you, but it was all a lie. It's so horrible. And so fucking unfair."

"I'm sorry. I . . ."

"Don't say anything." Dave sat on the side of the bed and stared into his coffee cup, hunched forward, away from him.

"I fell in love with you," Aaron said. "I have no idea why my brother hurt you the way he did or why he would even want to. I don't know why I feel responsible for that, but I do. I hoped . . . I hoped you'd never find out the truth. I'd hoped in the time we were together that Troy really had taken his own life."

"And now?" Dave's voice sounded ragged.

"Now I wish he'd killed us both."

Dave said nothing for a moment. He hadn't touched his coffee.

"You don't need to leave today. Stay another night. I don't mind having you here, but you realize, of course, it's temporary. I got your wallet and cards back from Matt who took them all from you. You can have whatever is in Troy's bank accounts. You can have his credit card. I'll help you get a car tomorrow then you should be on your way."

"Okay. That's more than fair." Aaron felt so wretched. He'd taken a few sips of coffee, but now he felt sick to his stomach. He got out of bed. He quickly put the cup on his bedside table and picked up the discarded towel from a chair by the bed, covering up his naked bottom.

"I've already seen it," Dave called out, but Aaron was too busy barfing into the toilet to respond. He shut the door on Dave's last words, locking the door. Some things a man just had to do in private.

Troy awoke to the sound of the coast guard's foghorn. It was a little after six, the sky a dark gray. Typical California coast. He was totally sucked in by the heaviest fog he'd seen in years. He couldn't decide if he wanted coffee or a beer but chose coffee since he had a long day ahead of him. Beer would have been great, would have taken the edge off the endless tension. He waited for the coffee to brew, enjoying the scent of it.

He opened the fridge. Empty. He wasn't sure what he'd

expected. He watched the coast guard boat circle past him.

Are they looking for me?

He experienced a moment of panic. *I've got to get a grip. Nobody knows I'm here.* He gave up on the coffee, anxious to get moving now. He went into the head, peering out of the small porthole but the coast guard had moved on. Probably just making their early morning rounds. *Phew.*

Troy had hidden the money in a false bottom in the cupboard underneath the bathroom vanity. It took some work with a screwdriver and a wrench, but he lifted the wooden flooring and found the money, safe and secure, still tied in plastic bundles. He was so relieved he began to laugh. He hammered the fake flooring back into place with the blunt end of the screwdriver and closed the cupboard doors.

He would go to the market and do a little shopping, then set sail as soon as he could. He needed gas, he needed water . . . He started to make a list of all the supplies he'd need.

Dave worried about Aaron, but when he checked on him a little while later, he was sleeping, though it didn't seem necessarily peaceful slumber. He wandered the house, not wanting to leave him alone, in case the guy robbed him blind.

He chastised himself. That wasn't Aaron's style. It was Troy's. Aaron had stolen a chance at happiness. He was guilty of that. In the short time he'd known the man, he'd been good and kind. Dave called his three scheduled clients and begged them all to let him reschedule for the following day, offering them free training sessions for their inconvenience.

The sooner Aaron was out of here, the sooner he could figure out where he'd move to next. He'd pack up and put the house on the market. He should really start looking for a new place to live, but the truth was, he liked the house. He *loved* the studio. He just couldn't handle such a huge mortgage on his own. It was extravagant and wasteful.

What he really wanted was the life he thought he had. With the man he thought was the new and improved Troy Mayer.

Manuela did not return to the house that day. Neither did Alberto. He wasn't surprised. They were immigrants who wanted to work, and worked hard for their money, but he was pretty sure the homeowner brandishing a gun and acting like a weirdo crossed all kinds of lines.

He made chicken soup for lunch, pleased with how well it turned out. Aaron looked pretty gruesome but perked up with some soup inside him.

"It's the pills," he said. "They've really done a number on me. That, and of course," he moved a finger from Dave to himself, "this has screwed me up royally."

He left the soup bowl on the tray and closed his eyes.

"I don't need to get a car," he said. "If you could drive me to the Greyhound Bus tomorrow, I'll be on my way. I just need a little more . . ."

He fell asleep before he could finish his sentence.

Dave called Darren Mayer, but the man wasn't answering any of his phones and his cell phone voicemail was full. What was going on with him? Downstairs in the living room, Dave turned on the TV to catch up on the news. Nancy's death had caused a minor sensation and had made the local news telecasts. The cops were being very tight-lipped about the details. Beyond saying the victim had been found strapped in the passenger seat, they released no more information. One local station featured a twenty-second sound bite from the Hidden Hills Police Department spokesman and a shot of Troy's trashed car, but other news had already begun to supersede the 'dead woman in the car.'

He zoned out watching the news and gave a start when a news bulletin flashed on CBS. There had been a fire in downtown LA. An entire historic warehouse had burned down. Police suspected arson.

Holy shit . . . Dave leaned forward. He knew the building. It was the Mayer family's building. He wondered if Darren had been in it. Would the thugs come to the house next? How long would it take for the police to figure out that Darren and Nancy were husband and wife, or did they already know?

Where was Troy? Was he alive or dead? He began to debate his feelings on the subject. When he dissected his roiling emotions, all he felt was fury. And stress. He couldn't bear anymore tension. He'd get Troy out of his life once and for all and Aaron out of his house. He'd start afresh . . .

He lay back on the sofa, his eyes drifting shut. So much tension. He tried to put himself into a relaxed state. All he saw in his mind was mirrors. In the mirrors were the two men he realized he had feelings for. He loved them both. Or he loved one. But which was which?

Dave fell into a restless sleep and awakened an hour later but that was only because Aaron shook him awake.

"The police are here," Aaron said, looking tense. "The warehouse burned down. They found my dad inside. They got him to UCLA but he died in the burn unit. We also lost one employee. Gloria Gilroy. Jesus Christ, Dave. They think the Santinis are coming for us next."

Troy shopped Albertson's supermarket on Quintana Road in Morro Bay, excited about his pending departure. He bought enough to last him a few weeks, loading up on long-life milk that would not taste as good as the fresh stuff, but would do in a pinch. He stared at the massive display of bananas, debating whether he should buy some. Not that he craved bananas, but there were so many he felt the urge to buy.

He was aware of a guy following him around the store. He was cute, all right. Troy enjoyed the familiar tug of desire in his groin and smiled back.

"Hey," the guy said.

"Hey." Troy smiled back as the grocery bagger threw his items into an array of bags.

"It *is* you, isn't it?" the guy said, walking outside with Troy.

Troy's heart dropped. "Me?" He tried to keep his tone nonchalant, but he was ready to run any second now.

"Aaron. C'mon, man, It's me, Jake. I know it's you."

Troy laughed. Aaron. Man, how ironic. This clown thought he was Aaron.

"Heck! I knew it was you. What are you doing up here? Got time for a coffee?"

"Not really," Troy said. This guy really was cute. He wondered if Aaron had been banging him but decided he hadn't. He didn't get the idea that his brother had given up his old life with a hot guy like this lurking anywhere near it.

"I didn't think you'd come back up here, but I'm hurt that you are but didn't call me."

The guy really did look sad.

"I'm sorry about that." Troy leaned in and kissed Jake on the lips.

"Whoa, Mary!" Jake recoiled instantly.

Troy shrugged. "Sorry, I couldn't resist."

The man looked astonished. "I had no idea you were gay. I mean, you always claimed not to be . . . you always claimed to be asexual more than anything."

Troy started to feel uncomfortable. Jake was getting a little hysterical.

"I'm sorry," he said again. "I just . . . always wanted to do that."

"You did?" They had reached the rental car Troy had driven up from LA. Troy started loading up the trunk.

"Listen, why didn't you ever tell me?" Jake asked, stepping in way too close for Troy's liking.

"I guess it took me a while to figure it out." That seemed

like a safe response.

"That's too bad," the other guy said. His hand came out of his pocket and he zapped Troy in the neck with a stun gun. The gun's rays were agonizing. Troy felt the pain in his nose and eyes. He could smell his own skin burning.

"Sorry, Aaron but the loan sharks took my dogs. They know I helped you get out of town and they want their money back or they're gonna kill my pets." He gave Troy a hard look as if waiting for him to challenge Jake's statement. Troy, however, was petrified. He couldn't speak. His heart raced so badly he thought he might be having a heart attack.

Jack grunted and pushed Troy into his trunk, slamming the lid down on him.

Troy lay, squashed in the back with most of his groceries. He was so terrified when the vehicle actually stopped that he peed his pants. His life flashed before his eyes when the lid was raised again and two of the meanest sons of bitches he'd ever seen in his life stared down at him.

"Bet you never thought you'd see us again," one of them leered. He cocked a gun. A scream died on Troy's trembling lips as the man dragged him out of the trunk, hurled Troy to his knees in front of him.

"You should've paid up Aaron," he said.

And then he pulled the trigger.

CHAPTER SIXTEEN

The police told Aaron and Dave that the Santini family's huge drug bust set up for Saturday night had gone haywire thanks to a police informant being outed.

The informant was . . . Darren Mayer.

Darren had agreed to cooperate with the authorities once he realized his own son, Troy Mayer, had become a double-dipping turncoat.

"We don't think Darren realized what a dangerous game he was playing," Detective Gregory Hills of the West Los Angeles division's fraud squad told Aaron.

"He agreed to hire Paulo Santini, thinking he could convince Paulo that he was on his team, meanwhile, he was reporting everything to us."

"How do you know I'm Aaron Mayer and not Troy?" Aaron asked.

"Your father told us. He said your behavior has been odd for a couple of weeks but after you stopped your best friend—or rather Troy's best friend Matt—from getting fleeced, he said he suspected it was you. When you were injured and your real identity came out at the hospital, he knew he was in big trouble."

Aaron sat back on the living room sofa, Dave sitting close to him.

"My father was your informant? He never said anything," Aaron said, glancing at Dave. "He cut me out of everything. Every single meeting. He worked behind my back."

Hills shrugged. "He was trying to solidify his position with the Santini family." He gave Aaron a disarming grin. "You really freaked him out firing Santini."

"Yeah, I knew that. He re-hired him as soon as he returned

from his honeymoon." Aaron paused. "Who killed Nancy? The Santini's or my brother?"

Neither detective said anything for a moment. Hills changed the subject.

"When did you last speak to your father, Aaron?"

Aaron thought for a moment. "When he called me and told me I had to come up with the money for the drugs."

"He came to the hospital when Aaron was admitted a couple of days ago," Dave said. "I will tell you, he was awful. He wasn't interested in getting to know the son he abandoned."

Aaron liked the look of fury on Dave's face. It seemed . . . protective somehow.

Detective Hills and his partner were sitting in chairs opposite Dave and Aaron.

"You have to understand . . . once he figured out you weren't Troy, he was screwed. We have no idea where the two million dollars belonging to the Santini family is. We offered your father protection, but he was scared."

"Frankly, I don't blame him," Detective Hills's partner said. Aaron scrambled to remember the guy's name.

"He thought he could just leave town. I mean he really planned on that. First his wife leaves him then he makes an arrangement to meet Paulo Santini at the warehouse."

This was a surprise. "He did?" Aaron asked.

"He called us and told us the meeting was taking place. He wasn't supposed to go there without one of us being with him."

"Oh, boy. That's why you think he's after me now . . . wait. Me, or Troy?"

Detective Hills gave him an appreciative look. "Troy. Problem is, the Santini family still thinks you're Troy Mayer. We haven't told anyone you're not him."

"So they're still after you." Dave's gaze on him was unsettling. Aaron felt a distinct chill. He'd be lucky if he *ever* got to spend another night under the same roof as Dave.

"With the killing of Darren Mayer and Gloria Gilroy . . . not to mention Nancy Mayer, the Santini family has canceled the shipment of drugs that was supposed to arrive in San Pedro Harbor on Saturday night. They're still going to be looking for you . . . and their money," Detective Hills said.

"What do we do?" Aaron noticed the sharp glance from Dave, which might as well have screamed, 'What do you mean we?' at Aaron.

"Keep a low profile for the next couple of days. We are looking for your brother and Paolo Santini. You're in the safest community in Los Angeles here and we will have a word with the guards on the gate not to let anybody in that they absolutely cannot verify as being residents, or legitimate visitors," Hill said.

"Do you have any idea where my brother is?" Aaron asked.

"We found out he rented a car shortly after he totaled his."

Aaron gaped at him. "He killed Nancy?"

"Looks that way."

"Good God," Dave said. He seemed to move an inch or two away from Aaron.

"Any idea where he went?"

"The rental agency says that the Lojack system has been activated . . . we got a few pings from his cell phone . . . we'll let you know."

"Okay, thanks." Aaron was a jumble of nerves. He might have been in a safe community but death and mayhem surrounded him and Dave. He didn't like it. He wanted Dave safe.

The cops told them to call with any questions or concerns . . . or in the unlikely event that Troy were to call them; they should let the detectives know.

As soon as they left, Aaron turned to Dave.

"How . . . does it make you feel knowing that they think it's unlikely that Troy will call you?"

"Don't know, to be honest."

That was a fair answer. Aaron had never felt so far away from Dave. It was killing him.

"Do you want me to leave tonight?"

"No." His voice came out a harsh bark. "We already discussed this. Tomorrow we'll get you a car and you can be on your way."

Aaron swallowed. "Okay."

Dave left him, sweeping out of the room and up the staircase. Aaron couldn't face another night alone in the bed, and yet, he needed to rest. He was in a lot of pain. He swallowed a couple of pills from the hospital. Oops. He saw, too late, he was supposed to take only one Norco every four to six hours. He sat on the sofa, not sure what to expect. He found it difficult to get comfortable as he channel surfed. His whole body ached. He hated what Matt had done to him but didn't blame the guy, actually.

He let out a sigh. It took the pills a whole hour to start to work. When they did, they were like little pieces of magic. He felt so good and so floaty, he no longer felt pain. All evening long, Dave kept waking him, asking him if he wanted food or drink. No. Aaron wanted to return to his wonderful land in his brain, a land where he and Dave were together, making love, laughing . . . feeding each other with their fingers.

Late that night, he came down off the Norco and the dull ache in his shoulder returned. He didn't want to take another pill. His stomach felt horrible. He foraged in the fridge for food, surprised when a sleepy Dave returned to the kitchen in his pajamas and offered to heat some soup.

"I knew you'd be hungry. I couldn't wake you up," he grumbled. He was so hot. He looked like a young Rock Hudson in his well-cut, expensive looking pajamas. Naked was better in Aaron's opinion but he liked knowing that Dave was naked under the pants. He could see his ass crack beneath the sheer fabric and imagined running his tongue along it.

He sat at the kitchen table, watching Dave move around the kitchen. He wished the man would turn around so he could get a good look at his crotch.

Dave caught him staring when he turned around to ask, "You want some melted cheese on it?" Aaron wanted to say yes, not because he really craved the cheese but because he would say and do anything to keep Dave with him a little longer.

"Yes, please."

Dave nodded, pulling cheese out of the fridge. Their silence was companionable and as Dave brought the soup bowl over to him, he glanced at the clock.

"You like the TV show *Friends*?"

"Sure."

"It's on. We could both do with a laugh. Then we should get some rest. We gotta get an early start car hunting in the morning."

Aaron nodded. He did not want to go car hunting. He wanted to go cock hunting in Dave's pajama pants. Being the congenial house guest however, he picked up his bowl and followed Dave into the living room again.

Dave handed him a glass of water and a napkin and sat on the other end of the sofa. So near, and yet so far away. The episode of the long-running sitcom was a poignant one. In it, the six friends imagine what their lives would have been like had they chosen different paths, the ones originally slated for them.

Aaron finished his soup wishing he could start again with Dave.

"Would you ever consider giving me a second chance?" he asked Dave, but when he looked across the sofa at the man he now knew he loved beyond all reason, he saw that Dave was asleep.

"We have tonight," he whispered, getting up, putting the soup bowl on the coffee table and picking up a cashmere throw from a wing chair. He covered up Dave then grabbed a second throw for himself. This wasn't as good as being naked in the man's arms, but it sure beat the stuffing out of sleeping in separate rooms.

Aaron turned off the TV, loving the sound of Dave's even breathing. He tried to ignore the screaming, fearful little voice in his brain. Nothing would happen to Dave. Nothing would go wrong. No Santinis. No bad car accidents . . . no raging fires.

He would get the new car and move on. He could stay some place close. He knew there was a building with furnished, executive-style apartments for rent on Sunset Boulevard in Brentwood. He'd passed them every day since he'd been here. He could hole up there and still be close to Dave. He could be as near as Dave would let him, maybe drive by to catch a glimpse of him from time to time.

God. Please. Let him change his mind about me . . .

Dave awoke early, looked beside him, seeking out . . .

Aaron.

God. I can't want him. The man is a lunatic. He lied to me. He's my husband's brother, for fuck's sake.

He leaned back against the sofa cushion. Why, oh why, in spite of the discomfort of not being nestled in thousand-thread count sheets and a duvet, had he had the best night's sleep in days?

Because I'm with him.

Stupid.

Yeah. Him and me.

He looked around outside the windows. Past dawn, it

looked like it was going to be a perfect day once the cloud cover burned off a little. Perfect time for a run. He felt nice and warm and debated over whether he should rouse himself. He pulled the throw covering him a little closer to his chin. He didn't recall getting up and retrieving it . . . must have been Aaron.

Damn.

Apart from lying about who he was, he had been amazing. He had been the most *honest* person he knew. He took a beating from Matt for fuck's sake.

God . . . where the hell was Troy? He had a bad feeling about his trigger-happy spouse. What if he came back with the Santinis and started shooting up the place? What the hell had compelled him to shoot Nancy? Why not just let her go if he didn't want her anymore? He still couldn't get his head around the idea of Troy liking women. No. Troy liked anyone who was useful to him. *I outlived my usefulness. He dropped me like a hot turd.*

He hated how he was feeling. Time for a run. He got up, instantly awakening Aaron whose eyes looked glazed with pain.

"Are you okay?" he asked him, reaching out a hand.

Aaron didn't respond.

"You slept on the wrong shoulder, fool." Dave said this kindly, getting up and resettling Aaron into a more comfortable position.

"Why didn't you get up and go to bed?"

"Because I wanted to be next to you. Dave, I'm so sorry about all of this."

"I know." Emotion cracked in Dave's voice. "Rest up now. I'll get you a pill."

"No. They're too strong."

"I'll give you some Motrin and a banana. You'll be okay. I'm going to take a run and come back and make you some breakfast. Okay?"

"Okay." Aaron's smile was shaky.

Dave sliced up a banana and brought it to Aaron with a couple of pills and a glass of water.

"It's so weird." Aaron frowned. "I kept dreaming of bananas. I had the strangest thoughts . . . that I was sorry I didn't buy them. Is that freaky, or what?"

Dave looked at him. "It's a good thing you're not taking any more Norco." He watched Aaron down the pills and sink back against the cushions.

"I wish I could come with you. I always want to run with you, but it seemed obvious Troy never asked and I was acting different enough as it was."

"You like to run?" Dave thought it was a shame that Aaron had to leave today. "You know . . . nothing about you added up, but somehow it seemed . . . right."

The words wavered between them for a moment. Dave wasn't going to give Aaron the chance to say anything that would play on his emotions.

He kept his tone business-like. "Well, you're in no fit shape to run right now. I won't be long."

Aaron had turned his face away. It seemed all crumpled. "Okay," he said again. Dave suspected he was crying.

Outside the house, Dave looked up and down the street. He turned left and ran farther up the hilly road to Strada Vecchia, the most expensive street in Los Angeles. He had a magnificent view of the Los Angeles basin below him as his worked his way up the mountain. He heard a noise in some bushes and stopped.

A fawn stumbled out of the thick underbrush onto the road. She was a beauty. Deer, coyote, possums, squirrels, ravens, mountain lions, bobcats, and even wolves were not unusual in this untamed paradise. Being a private road, these wild animals were safer than most since the people in the neighborhood respected them. These beautiful creatures had more to fear from starvation thanks to long stretches of drought in the hills. Poachers' snares sometimes got them . . . and, of course, rattle snakes, which seemed to multiply by the day.

He pushed his body hard, enjoying the pain with the increased stress on his muscles. He lost track of time as he slipped between two eucalyptus trees that were the only indications of a foot trail deep in the heart of the Santa Monica Mountains.

By the time he'd returned, drenched but totally calm, he was astonished to find Aaron kneeling beside Nikko Watanabe in their neighbor's yard, tending his Zen garden.

"What's going on?" Dave asked, wiping the sweat from his brow.

"Can you believe it? Somebody stomped all over his garden and totally wrecked the flow of his stones," Aaron said, looking over his shoulder at Dave. He looked so upset, Dave didn't know how to respond.

"It's true," Nikko said, leaning back on his haunches. "I came out just now and saw the mess. I knew Troy would understand and he's been awesome."

"But . . ." Dave's voice trailed off. Aaron had a broken hand and a busted-up shoulder but here he was helping out a neighbor. A man that in the past, Troy — the real Troy — had tormented.

"It's okay," Aaron said, in soothing tones. "We can fix this."

Dave watched the two bent heads working as the men's hands stroked the tiny pebbles with small wooden rakes.

Aaron and Nikko worked in unison. Dave moved around, catching a glimpse of Aaron's pained expression. He was about to say something when Nikko said, "Who would do this? Who would mess with my chi like this?"

"Your chi?" Dave knew the meaning of spiritual energy

but was only beginning to understand the reverence with which Aaron was raking the stones. "You're making such a beautiful pattern," he said. "They look like ripples of water."

"Exactly," Nikko said. "I'm just so grateful Troy was willing to help."

"Of course I'm willing to help!"

Dave watched a minute or two more, hypnotized by the rhythmic movements.

"You have no idea," Aaron suddenly said, looking over his shoulder again at Dave, "This could send Nikko's karma into a yin yang whirlwind!"

Dave had no idea what the heck *that* meant but gleaned it wasn't a good thing. "You can't work with that hand, sweetie. Here, let me help. Just tell me what to do."

"Three's a good number," Nikko muttered.

"Powerful. Solidifies intention," Aaron agreed.

Dave wondered how the hell he hadn't met Aaron sooner. Where had he been all this time? Oh, yeah. Living a hellish existence. He tried not to worry about the damage the man might be doing to his hand and shoulder.

When they finished raking the stones into the correct pattern, Nikko went into the house and came out with some incense and a small bell and chanted a few words.

"Come inside for breakfast," he insisted.

Aaron and Dave exchanged enquiring glances.

"Come on you two, it's a fair exchange for helping my chi." He grinned at Aaron. "And my karma. And by the way, I'm a damned good cook."

Dave stood and helped a wobbly Aaron to his feet.

"Are you okay?" he asked Aaron.

"Yes, I'm fine. Thank you."

"I have some Rescue Remedy and some wonderful hibiscus tea," Nikko said, ushering them inside after they'd all removed their shoes and left them outside.

Nikko's house was very Asian, or as he called it, tropical Asian. Large, clear vases of red ginger and, as Aaron correctly identified them, *obake* anthurium decorated every room they passed.

"*Obake* is Japanese for ghost," Aaron said. "These anthurium are sacred to ancient deities." He seemed to notice the astonished look on Nikko's face.

"Okay," Nikko said. "What the fuck is going on? Who are you?"

Dave froze. Nikko laughed. He was only joking. He felt Aaron tense beside him, but Nikko had said it in jest and as they all took turns washing their hands from the garden work, Nikko insisted they sit and let him handle breakfast on his own. He prepared French toast, waffles and scrambled egg whites and kept making cracks about how nice Troy was underneath his mean exterior.

Neither Dave nor Aaron said much. Aaron was in pain. David could tell, but Aaron kept a brave face on things. Nikko kept plying him with herb teas and tinctures and between that and the excellent food, Aaron seemed to relax a little.

Dave too, drank the hibiscus tea, stunned when Nikko said, "It's excellent for sexual problems."

"What?" Dave almost scolded his tongue.

Nikki shrugged. "I can read your energy. Some real healing energy trapped inside him." He pointed a finger at Aaron. "I mean look at him. A broken hand, a broken shoulder . . ." Nikko frowned. "He has no support." He shot Dave an accusatory glance. "I hope you go home and spend some time reawakening your kundalini and unleash your inner fire. You will recover such vitality." His gaze seared into Dave's, then Aaron's, and back again.

"Don't worry about the dishes. Just go make love. Embrace the microcosmic orbit and be happy."

"Sounds good to me," Aaron said. He looked at the table.

Dave couldn't believe the man had said that.

Nikko raised a brow in Dave's direction.

"Thanks for breakfast," Dave said. He stood and helped Aaron to his feet. They left the house. Outside, they stuffed their feet into their shoes and shuffled down the path. Dave had to admit they'd made the Zen garden look amazing.

He didn't say a word until they were back inside their house.

"Do you have any idea what he was talking about?" Dave asked.

"No." Aaron glanced away. "It made my cock hard, though."

Dave stared at him a moment, then threw his head back and laughed. This ignited Aaron's laughter, too.

Dave moved closer. Aaron met his eyes. "Take me in your arms, kiss me."

Dave wrapped his arms around him. He seemed hesitant but his mouth gradually found Aaron's.

"We've got to get some of that tea," a breathless Aaron said, between kisses.

"Yeah," Dave smiled, "And figure out what the hell a microcosmic orbit is."

"Oh, I know what that is already," Aaron stroked his hair.

"You do?" Dave kissed him again, relaxing.

"Yeah. I experience one every time you touch me."

That did it. Those few words sent Dave into a frenzy. He picked up Aaron and carried him upstairs. He had to set the man down gently on the bed and undress him—with difficulty. It wasn't terribly elegant love since the man had pillows cushioning his injured body parts, but somehow it turned into one of the most tender and most pleasurable lovemaking sessions Dave had ever experienced.

Aaron's cock kept jutting into his face as he moved around the man's prone, squirming body trying to get his attention.

Each time their mouths met in a heated kiss, Aaron's cock seemed to leak a little more.

"I'm sorry," they both said in unison.

"Fuck," Dave said, glancing down at the hard cock in his hand as he knelt between Aaron's parted thighs. His mouth sought out the cockhead now scraping along his chin.

Aaron moaned as Dave sucked him in, taking him an inch at a time until he reached the base of the man's cock. Aaron's balls delighted him. The sac showed off the nuggets beneath them to full advantage and Dave took them into his hand, coming off Aaron's cock briefly to massage them with his tongue and lips. Aaron's ass flew off the bed and he had to press the man back down to the sheets again. He lifted his head, smiled at Aaron and swallowed his cock once more.

With a rousing cry, Aaron came and so did Dave, all over his boxer briefs. Not that Dave cared. When Aaron urged him to remove them, the man begged him for his cock. Dave let Aaron swab him with his tongue.

As he began to soften, Dave fell back against the pillows beside Aaron. They smiled at each other, drifting off into a pleasant nap, face to face, their legs entangled around one another.

Aaron couldn't believe it when he woke up an hour later with Dave lying beside him. Dave stirred as soon as Aaron did.

"We should shower," Dave said.

Aaron's heart sank. Damn. He wants to go car shopping. "Okay."

As he tried to get out of the bed, Dave put a restraining hand on him.

"No, sweetie, let me help you." Dave scooted to the side of the bed and helped him stand. "How are you feeling?"

"Good. Much better. How about you?"

"Yeah. Dammit. I think that freaky actor might have a few points about cosmic orbits."

They walked into the bathroom together. Dave turned on the taps. "We need to cover your cast in plastic." He ran his hand under the water spray to check the temperature. "And if it's okay with you, first thing tomorrow, I'm filing for a divorce." He flicked a glance at Aaron who couldn't help the smile spreading across his face.

"If that's okay with you." Dave's mouth quirked into a grin.

"Very okay with me." Aaron leaned in for another kiss.

After the kind of lengthy shower that would give environmentalists fits, the two men dried off and in spite of good intentions to talk and clean the already clean house, they fell into bed again. They spent all day making love, eating good food and watching Johnny Depp movies on their cable company's pay-on-demand channel lineup.

They fell asleep, awakening early the next morning.

"I missed you," Dave said as he yawned and stretched.

Aaron had missed him, too. He leaned over for a kiss, disappointed that Dave wanted to go for a run.

"We should make a list of things we need to do," Dave said as he pulled on sweats.

Aaron got out of bed and threw on jeans. "I'm gonna make some coffee and get started on the list," he said.

They walked downstairs, kissing each other at the bottom. Dave reached into a bowl on the table by the door and extracted his keys. "I won't be long, babe. Wish you'd wait in bed for me."

"I'll make a cup of coffee and go right back up there."

They grinned at each other. Dave went out the door, Aaron turning to head to the kitchen. He didn't get far. Seconds later, he heard a gunshot. In rapid succession, he heard two more and a man's voice screaming.

Aaron's mind went blank. He turned and ran, tripping on the two stairs outside the front door. Some maniac stood in their garden firing at Dave who was on his knees, trying to duck for cover.

Without even thinking, Aaron threw himself over Dave, flattening the man underneath him on the dew-covered grass. Aaron was convinced he would die, but better him than his beloved Dave. He shouted, "Dave, I love you," waiting for the bullet that would tear them apart once and for all.

The bullet came, but Aaron didn't feel it. He heard it.

He raised his head and looked up to see mild-manned Nikko Watanabe with a smoking gun looking down on the sprawled body of one dead bad guy.

It was only when Aaron stood that he got a good look at him and recognized Paulo Santini.

"We are leaving this house today," a shaky Dave said. "Are you crazy or something? You could have gotten killed!"

Aaron just looked at him. He knew that in different circumstances . . . any circumstances, he'd do it again, too.

CHAPTER SEVENTEEN

The two detectives returned to the house twenty minutes later. The media arrived in full force, helicopters whirring overhead. It wasn't every day a TV star murdered a Mafioso — in crime-free Bel Air — protecting his neighbor.

Dave, Aaron and Nikko all corroborated one another's stories. Not that they needed to. They had been able to piece it together via eye-witness testimony and taped evidence from three different neighbors.

Santini had somehow crept past the gate guard as his accomplice, Joe Carson, distracted him with a long tale. This gave Santini ample time to reach Dave and Troy's house.

Dave watched footage of Aaron covering his body to shield him from gunshots.

"Brave guy," Detective Hills said. Aaron still didn't know his partner's name and was too embarrassed to ask.

"We do have more news," Hills said. "We found your brother's body in the trunk of his rental car. He'd been badly beaten, his face smashed to pulp."

"Oh, my God," Aaron said. He looked at Dave. "I'm so sorry."

Dave nodded. For a moment, he didn't say anything. "I'm glad it wasn't you. Where was he?" he asked Hills.

Hills looked bewildered. "That's what's weird. He was in the parking lot of an Albertson's store in Morro Bay. There's a bank across the road. Their surveillance footage shows him and another man talking by the open trunk. The man appears to stun-gun him and pushes him into the trunk, closes it, and drives off."

His partner jumped in, earning a disgruntled look from Hills. "About half an hour later, we see another guy dropping the car off again."

Aaron stared at them. "Any idea who they were?"

"We've been showing the freeze-frame photos on the northern California coastal town stations. The second man appears to be a local loan shark, Ernie Torres."

"Oh, shit." Aaron was mortified. "Those guys tortured and beat me, burned my car down. They probably thought Troy was me."

The detectives said they would organize snapshots of the men in question to see if he recognized the first man from the bank's camera images.

"Any idea what your brother was doing in Morro Bay?" Hills asked.

"Yes. He has a boat there. The Promise. You say he was at a grocery store? Maybe he was buying food and planning to get out of town."

The detectives eventually left. "Think the Santinis will leave us alone now?" Aaron asked Dave.

"No. And I think it's time we blew this Popsicle stand. We should go to Hawaii. I own a house in Kauai, on the North Shore. It's a little beach cottage. It's absolutely beautiful there and secluded. We could take the boat and just go."

"Think we can do that? Really?"

"Why not?

Fourteen Months later . . .

Sometimes, when Aaron thought about it, the past year or so had been total bliss. He and Dave were more in love than ever. They got along great and had opened three yoga studios on the island of Kauai that were successful and popular, but sometimes, he felt as if he was on borrowed time.

"We all are," Dave said, whenever Aaron confessed that he felt as if he'd stolen his brother's life. He hadn't. Troy had thrown away everything he should have held dear. He'd left a trail of broken hearts behind him. He'd hurt so many people who'd genuinely cared for him.

The cops had gone over the boat inch by inch, but the money Troy stole was never recovered. The Santini family had been forced to give up hunting down Troy since he was dead and now half the mob family was on trial.

Jake, a longtime friend of Aaron's, turned out to be the one who'd tasered Troy, and delivered him into the hands of the loan sharks. He had good reason—his hostage dogs—but Aaron wanted to leave the past behind him. It was just him and Dave now.

The future was theirs. On a balmy Sunday afternoon, they decided to take the boat out around the island. The annual Festival of the Canoes would soon start, when locally made vessels in the ancient tradition would make a slow pilgrimage to Polynesia the way navigators of old did, via the constellations. No computers, compasses . . . nothing.

Dave and Aaron packed a picnic lunch. They'd debated inviting friends, but as usual, cherished the idea of being alone together. Dave went into the galley to organize some finger foods.

The boat rocked on the water as if it were made of paper. The wind swirled around him in a haze and whipped his fair hair around his face. Desperately, Aaron tried to see through waves rising and falling around him. *Troy? Troy?* A mix of anxious anticipation and dread filled his rapidly beating heart as he scanned the water. The boat took on a life of its own and attempted to wrestle him over the side, propelling him into the unknown depths. *Come. Come with me, Aaron.* A face looked up at him now in the swirling water. It was *his.*

"Babe?" Dave asked. "Why are you leaning down so far? One fast wave and I'll lose you."

Dave pulled him back, looking shaken.

"You can't lose me. When we get back, I want to sell this boat. I hate it. It has bad vibes."

"We should refurbish it."

"Yeah. We could do that." Aaron sipped at the glass his lover handed him. "But right now, I really want to fuck you."

"My, my. And miss the canoe race?"

"Fuck the canoe race. We have microcosmic orgasms to navigate."

"Nikko's gonna be sore as hell if we don't watch his canoe launch."

Aaron grinned. "Nope. He's gonna be more pissed if we block our chi again."

"True." Dave kissed him. "Last one into bed has to do exactly what the other one wants."

He turned, but neither moved.

Dave laughed. "You're no fun."

"I want to do to you whatever you want me to do."

Dave sipped his champagne. "Me, too."

Aaron frowned. "You go first then. What do you want?"

"I want to sit on the deck, watching the canoes with you sitting on my lap, my cock buried deep inside you."

Aaron dropped to his knees, his champagne keeling over the edge of his glass. He unfastened the buttons on his lover's jeans, liberating his cock. He stuffed it into his mouth, Dave looking down at him, stroking his head.

"Beautiful," he murmured.

Aaron slid his lover's jeans down his tanned thighs, Dave kicking them off his feet.

"Get up," Dave instructed.

Aaron rose. Dave walked behind him and with one arm around Aaron's body, rubbed against him from behind. Other boats surrounded them and the people on them could probably see everything, but Aaron didn't care. He felt Dave's fingers on his fly and hastily pushed down his pants. Dave knelt behind him, his tongue roaming his ass crack, delving deeper into him. Aaron bent forward a little. He clutched the boom, causing them both to sway as Dave began sucking his ass.

Dave, impatient, pushed Aaron toward the bench seat. He turned Aaron around and as Aaron sat, facing him, Dave knelt, pulling off Aaron's pants. He held his ankles up and out, his tongue going back to Aaron's ass. Aaron could hear whistles and cheering but he had no idea if people were reacting to them or the canoes. Dave was impatient. He sat beside Aaron who climbed onto his lap. He straddled Dave's thighs as Dave rubbed his cock along Aaron's asshole.

"Stick it in," Aaron moaned.

Dave took his time since they had no lube. The boat rocked, but Aaron was no longer tormented by the past. He wasn't fearful of the future. He was not alone anymore. He'd found his man, the one that ultimately his brother—his broken half—had led him to. Maybe Troy had always known Aaron could love Dave enough for both of them. As Dave finally slammed his cock into Aaron and fucked him, Aaron gave himself up to his lover's insistent thrusts.

Troy would no longer hurt or haunt him. He would not feel guilty one more day. He would live . . . for both of them. For all of them. He would live without mirrors, loving Dave.

Face to face.

One on one.

Without limits.

No recriminations.

No regrets.

"Fuck me harder," he shouted into the wind. Dave held Aaron's hips and gave it to him. Good and hard.

You may also enjoy the following from eXtasy Books Inc:

Man in the Mirror
A.J. Llewellyn and D.J. Manly

Excerpt

He would drop off the last guests leaving that morning, and Aaron would work on cleaning the common areas and the last guest room, Plumeria, which mercifully required just cleaning and fresh sheets. Once again, he ran through his checklist of all the extras they provided for their clientele. The mystery man who'd booked this room wouldn't give them his name. He'd booked through Pleasant Holidays and his package included a rental car.

I wonder who the hell he is and what the big mystery is. He can't be some big movie star. He would have booked a cottage.

Aaron heard the car drive up as he gave the room one final critical once-over and grabbed a fresh plumeria lei from the fridge, then walked outside to greet their guest.

"My God! Nikko!" Aaron shouted with joy at the welcome sight of their former neighbor from Bel Air. Nikko Watanabe, a TV actor, had stayed in touch with Aaron and Dave who had rented out their house back in LA. He hugged Aaron hard. When Dave came around the corner with John and Albert's luggage, he dropped the bags and hurried to their friend, who gave him a hug too.

Nikko stared at them. "Married life in paradise suits you," he said.

"Man, it's good to see you!"

Aaron bid him an Aloha and gave him his lei greeting, slipping the fragrant flowers over Nikko's head and around his neck. Quickly hugging John and Albert goodbye, a strange feeling of panic enveloped him as he took Nikko to his room. The actor raved over the sumptuous island furniture, the vintage bric-a-brac, and the flip flops with a samurai sword embellishment.

"The agent at Pleasant Holidays said you love samurai stuff. I never guessed it was you!" Aaron said.

Nikko laughed. "I swore her to secrecy. I love this attention to detail. It's so you!"

It was him. Aaron loved taking care of their guests.

"I want to try new things this trip." Nikko leaned back, relaxing in the big wing chair by the windows. "I've been reading about Kipu Falls. Do you recommend them?"

Aaron stifled a groan. He loved people exploring his precious island, but he hated that visitors had begun finding out about secret places in the islands thanks to an irresponsible collection of books the locals disparagingly called The Blue Book. The authors not only gave detailed directions to hidden gems that only locals had been privy to, but apparently didn't care that many required trespassing on private property.

The outer islands were filled with people who were a bit, well, quirky, who prized their solitude and the untouched splendor of Kauai above all else. Suddenly they were being subjected to hundreds of people each and every week parading through their properties to get to 'hidden Kaui.'

Aaron and Dave had heard all the stories and tried to discourage their guests from partaking of illegal activities. Kipu Falls in particular was a raw wound. Two young women had read The Blue Book and had come to the garden island and followed the directions to it. They saw a trespassing sign at the main dirt road and chose an unmarked path instead. Within seconds, they had no idea they were on the edge of an obscured cliff and fell to their deaths.

Their parents had come to Kauai, grief stricken. Aaron would never forget the pain and suffering he saw in their faces.

"It's dangerous," he told Nikko. "Ten people have died there."

"So I've heard." Nikko's gaze held a defiant gleam. Oh, boy.

"And Queen's Bath. What do you know of it?"

"You have to be a strong swimmer. The tides are rough. We've had a few tragedies there, too."

"I love a challenge." Nikko grinned at him. Aaron returned his smile, left Nikko to his own devices, and went to the living room, straightening it one more time. In the kitchen, he sat at the table making a list of the canapés he would serve with drinks. Since Dave was picking up a lot of stuff they needed, he would wait before preparing anything.

In the meantime, he checked emails, made notes of their new reservations. They had bookings through the New Year. He checked Yelp and TripAdvisor for their customer reviews. Nothing he needed to respond to. Yet. He wondered what the heck Steve and Eileen would say.

That reminded him. He signed onto the Yahoo group he and the other B and B owners had formed and warned them about the couple. I have photos, he posted. I'll put them in the database later.

He shut down the computer and walked along the path outside to Mr. Race's room. He knocked on the door, introduced himself, and prepared to apologize if the man had noticed any discrepancies with what he'd seen online versus the actual appearance of his accommodations.

The author was effusive in his praise and said, "I never, ever want to go home."

They all said that, and it was balm to Aaron's anxious state. After Mr. Race assured him he had everything he needed, Aaron continued on his way and walked past Rod and Wendy's cottage where he could hear the religious CD playing. Rod played it all day long.

Aaron crossed over to his herb and salad garden, cutting and pulling what he needed for their little drinks party that night. He and Dave only provided breakfast but as a personal gesture of hospitality, kept chilled, homemade coconut water and chilled cucumber water available for their guests in the dining room. It was another one of their little touches their visitors raved about.

He was in the kitchen a couple of hours later, cleaning and organizing food, when Dave arrived, saying, "Can I kidnap my husband for a quick lunch?"

Aaron laughed. "Of course you can." He helped Dave stow the food in the fridge and pantry and walked outside, slid his zoris onto his feet, and got into the car.

They held hands the whole way to the Ching Young Village. They loved the sushi bar there, but as they entered the sweeping shopping center with its vintage-looking red roofs, he thought about how they used to tear around the island to get their tasks accomplished. They'd learned the art of slow shopping here. It was a way of life.

"Mind if we take a quick look inside the Flop Shop?" he asked.

"Nope. I never mind," Dave said, as they went inside. Aaron checked their new arrivals and picked up the few sizes of flip flops missing from his stash, plus a few new embellishments. He was astonished when he approached the service desk to see the new neighbor — what was his name . . . Randy — talking to Dave.

"Hello again," Aaron said.

Randy smiled. "I have almost no food and thought I'd come and check this place out. Your chef told me this is the place to go — that I'd find anything I wanted here."

Aaron felt a chill go through him. Why was Randy looking at Dave when he said that? Aaron saw the crimson flush on his husband's face. It's not my imagination. He's making a pass at my husband!

Dave insisted on using his credit card for Aaron's purchases and after an awkward silence, the two men left the store.

"See you this evening!" Randy trilled.

I do not like that man," Aaron said when they were out of hearing.

"Randy? Oh, he's harmless."

Aaron didn't say anything. There was something about Randy Carlton that just really set him on edge.

"Sweetie, are you jealous?" Dave pulled him to him and gave him a quick kiss. "Don't be. I love you to bits. And besides, he seems really rather sweet. I guess he'll keep you on your toes."

Aaron turned and found the man not far behind them. Is he following us? When he saw Randy walk into a coffee shop, he let out a breath.

I'm too suspicious. I gotta calm down. Dave's right. He's just lonely and needs friends. He hugged Dave back and tried not to worry, tried not to stress. He looked back over his shoulder, relieved to find that his creepy new neighbor was nowhere in sight.

ABOUT THE AUTHOR

A.J. Llewellyn is the author of over three hundred published gay romance novels. A.J. lives in California, but dreams of living in Hawaii. Frequent trips to all the islands, bags of Kona coffee in the fridge and a healthy collection of Hawaiian records keep A.J. refueled.

Her passion for the islands led to writing a play about the last ruling monarch of Hawaii, Queen Lili'uokalani. A.J. has written a non-erotic novel about the overthrow of her kingdom written in diary form from her maid's point of view.

A.J. never lacks inspiration for male/male erotic romances and has to prise her fingers from the computer keyboard to pursue other passions: collecting books on Hawaiiana, surfing and spending time with family, friends and animal companions.

D.J. Manly: I write not only for my own pleasure but for the pleasure of my readers. I can't remember a time in my life when I haven't written and told stories. When I'm not writing, I'm dreaming about writing, doing something wild and adventurous, or trying to make the world a better and more open-minded place to live in. I adore beautiful men, and I know I'm not alone in this! Eroticism between consenting adults, in all its many forms, is the icing on the cake of life!

D.J. has published well over two hundred novels/novellas and is a well-seasoned writer.

www.ingramcontent.com/pod-product-compliance
Lightning Source LLC
Chambersburg PA
CBHW060812120626
46557CB00001B/189